"Sort of dangerous up here, isn't it?"

He didn't look down, but focused on Caley's eyes glittering in the moonlight. Talk about dangerous.

"The view is great." She gestured to the sky. "It was one of the things I'd missed about country life."

He felt himself being pulled in, like a moth to a lit candle. Against his will. Fascinated. Yet destined to get burned. "What else did you miss?"

"Peace and quiet. And space."

"So why'd you leave?"

"Long story."

Closed door on that topic. Probably for the best. He didn't need to carry her secrets, even if some deep-rooted part of him wanted to.

"I better get back. Have a good night."

"You, too. See you tomorrow." Caley smiled her goodbye, but didn't make a move to go inside. She remained staring at the stars.

Leaving Brady to wish, as he ambled away, that he could see what she did.

Books by Betsy St. Amant

Love Inspired

Return to Love
A Valentine's Wish
Rodeo Sweetheart
Fireman Dad
Her Family Wish
The Rancher Next Door

BETSY ST. AMANT

loves polka-dot shoes, chocolate and sharing the good news of God's grace through her novels. She has a bachelor's degree in Christian communications from Louisiana Baptist University and is actively pursuing a career in inspirational writing. Betsy resides in northern Louisiana with her husband and daughter and enjoys reading, kickboxing and spending quality time with her family.

The Rancher Next Door

Betsy St. Amant

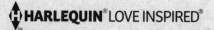

HARLEQUIN® LOVE INSPIRED®

Recycling programs
for this product may
not exist in your area.

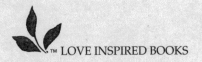

™ LOVE INSPIRED BOOKS

ISBN-13: 978-0-373-81688-0

THE RANCHER NEXT DOOR

www.LoveInspiredBooks.com

Printed in U.S.A.

Therefore, since we are receiving a kingdom which cannot be shaken, let us have grace, by which we may serve God acceptably with reverence and godly fear. For our God *is* a consuming fire.

—*Hebrews* 12:28,29

To my husband, Brandon, who is both a cowboy and a fireman. I get the best of both worlds! I love you.

In memory of Rodney Roach—
beloved rancher who fought the good fight
and is now saddlin' up in heaven.

Acknowledgments

Special thanks to my agent, Tamela Hancock Murray, for her constant support and belief in me, and to my editor, Emily Rodmell, for always knowing just where to take my stories to make them better! Also a sincere thank-you to my mother for being the world's greatest Nana and giving me so many free hours of babysitting so I can write and stay somewhat sane. Thanks to my fabulous critique partner Georgiana, for catching all the typos I miss and letting me know when my characters get bloody lips or whiplash (wink). And as always, thanks to my bestie Lori, who has brainstormed more than one novel with me while we sit on the kitchen floor and toss bouncy balls to our kids from four states away.

Chapter One

Caley Foster really wanted to put out a fire.

Or, for that matter, do anything more exciting than unload the rest of the boxes secured in the back of her beat-up red truck.

But that wasn't going to happen today. With a resigned sigh, Caley hiked one booted foot on the tire, shimmied over the edge of the truck and landed with a thump in the bed crammed full of boxes and tubs. She'd have thought after living in nine different cities in the past three years that she'd be used to moving by now—but this time felt different. Maybe because this time, she had to stay awhile.

Too bad whoever said you can't go home again hadn't meant it literally.

Caley's two-year-old black Labrador barked at her from the driveway as she began to shove yet another box across the rusted bed toward the open tailgate. "Scooter, like I told you before, it's going to take me a while to find the dog biscuits." She grunted as the box caught on an exposed bolt, and pushed again. Some days she almost regretted rescuing the hyper stray from a warehouse fire. But it was nice to take a friendly face along on her many travels, one who actually seemed to understand her.

Scooter barked again, and she wrinkled her nose at him. "Be patient, unless you want to do this work yourself."

A sudden giggle floated on the breeze toward Caley and wrapped around her ears like a cozy set of muffs. She glanced up with surprise, midpush, just in time to see a young blonde girl perched on the fence dividing her meager property from the sprawling acres of the Double C Ranch next door—and just in time to send her cardboard box tumbling over the edge of the tailgate.

Caley winced. Hopefully that wasn't the kitchenware, though it wouldn't have been the first time after a move that she ended up at the discount store searching for dinner plates. She slid her petite frame off the tailgate and righted the box on the ground.

The girl timidly hopped off the fence and approached her. "Do you need help? Did anything break?" Her blue eyes widened with worry, and she twisted a long strand of hair anxiously around one finger as if she thought the accident was her fault.

Caley straightened and smiled at the girl, who looked about ten or eleven years old. The golden years. It was sweet of her to be concerned. "It's all good. Thankfully, this was a box of pillows." She rummaged through it one more time to be sure. "And apparently an apron. And a bird feeder." She winked. "No wonder the box wasn't labeled."

The girl laughed again, and the sound warmed her heart. She'd missed being around kids. Her days spent nannying to earn a paycheck through college felt longer than just five years ago. It'd been nice to get an inside glimpse into families during that time—healthy, functioning families, that was.

A pinch of regret started in Caley's stomach, and she shook her head to dislodge it. No use dredging up the past. She was back in Broken Bend, Louisiana, to enjoy the remaining years she had with her grandmother while Nonie occupied the nursing home, and Caley would do exactly that. No more regrets.

If she started thinking on those, she might never stop.

"Scooter, look." Caley produced his sought-after box of canine treats from under a pillow and shook it. The eager dog pressed against her shins and barked, tail wagging hard enough to leave a bruise on her leg. She glanced at her new neighbor. "Want to feed him?"

The girl lit up with a bright smile, then hesitated, her grin fading as she looked over her shoulder toward the fence. "I probably shouldn't."

"Why not? He won't bite, I promise." She held out the box in one hand and offered a handshake with the other. "I'm Caley Foster. Looks like I'll be your neighbor for a while. I'm just renting, though." Why she felt the urge to clarify that to a kid, she wasn't sure. Maybe for her own benefit. *Temporary. Always temporary.* Though this time, temporary held no definite boundaries. She'd be here as long as her grandma needed her—even if Broken Bend was the last place she had ever hoped to land again.

"I'm Ava. My dad owns the Double C Ranch." Ava shook Caley's hand, then pointed with one skinny arm behind her to the property on the other side of the fence.

"It's beautiful." Caley took in the rolling fields and the tree-studded landscape, the crimson-and-gold-toned leaves offering a stark contrast to the bareness of Caley's plain half-acre lot. It'd have been nice to rent a bigger place while she was here, but at least she'd have some scenery next door to borrow. Hopefully Scooter wouldn't be too tempted to play in greener pastures. She nudged him with her foot. "You sure you don't want to feed him?"

Scooter barked again at the shaking of the treat box, and warmth slowly took over the wary look in Ava's eyes as he pressed his black nose against her hand. "Maybe just one treat wouldn't hurt."

"I'm positive he agrees with you." Caley dug a bone-shaped cookie from the box and handed it to Ava, who offered it to Scooter. He gulped it down quickly, blinking afterward as if wondering where it'd gone.

"He's so cute. I love animals." Ava tentatively patted Scooter's head. "I thought Labs were bigger?"

"Scooter must have been the runt of his family. Or maybe he's not a purebred." She shrugged with a smile. "Either way, he makes up for his smaller size with heart."

Ava rubbed him a little harder, and Scooter immediately leaned against her jeans-clad shins and whined deep in his throat.

"He's shameless." She laughed and rustled the fur on his back. "And spoiled. He'll stay like that forever if you keep petting him."

"I wish I could." Ava glanced toward her ranch, then back at Caley. "My dad has a bunch of animals, but doesn't let me do much with them. Says it's too dangerous."

That sounded familiar. Growing up, everything

under the sun was dangerous, according to Caley's father. Animals. Carnival rides. Staying out past nine o'clock at night even after she had her license. Then again, maybe Ava's father only owned high-strung Thoroughbreds or bulls. Most men had reasons to be protective.

Just not her dad.

"We have a bull, some cows, horses, a couple of foals and a few chickens." Ava crouched down to pet Scooter more thoroughly. "But I'm not allowed to help feed them or anything. I wish I could. Ever since Mom died…" Her voice trailed off and she buried her face in Scooter's floppy ears.

Empathy filled Caley's heart. Apparently she and her young neighbor had a lot more in common than just a love for animals. Although Caley wasn't sure if her mom still walked the earth or not. She briefly touched the girl's hair, warm from the autumn sunshine spilling through the tree limbs. "I'm sorry to hear that. You're welcome to play with Scooter anytime you'd like."

"As long as it's okay with her father, of course." A deep baritone sounded from the other side of the fence, and Caley jerked, spilling the box of biscuits. Scooter barked and scurried to eat them as Ava's face waxed pale.

"Hi, Dad." Ava winced and stepped away from Scooter. "I was just about to say that."

"You know you're not supposed to cross this

fence without permission." Ava's father, dressed in a plaid work shirt, faded jeans with dirt on the knees and equally muddy boots, strode across the short driveway toward them. A cowboy hat perched atop dark hair that peeked and curled from under the brim. He drew near and a smile broke the stubble on his tanned face, lightening the mood. Caley could almost tangibly feel Ava relax, as if the smile meant she wouldn't be in trouble. "Brady McCollough. And you are?"

"Your new neighbor, Caley Foster." She shook his hand, noticing the calluses on his palm, and quickly bent to scoop up the dog treats Scooter hadn't yet devoured. Hopefully Brady wouldn't see the color she knew burned her cheeks like a birthmark. She'd always blushed easily, but a man hadn't had this effect on her at close range in quite a while. She didn't remember him from her school days—and she was pretty sure she'd have remembered a face like that.

"Welcome to the neighborhood." Brady hooked one thumb in his belt buckle and draped his other arm casually around Ava. "Though it's not much of one. Your house and mine are the only ones for a few miles. The ranch next door to us has the next hundred acres, and his house is down the way."

Caley bit back a smile. She might not have missed much about Broken Bend when she left ten years ago, but the Southern accents might make the list next time. She hadn't heard such a lazy drawl in a while. "Good to know. I'm used to being alone, though." Nothing new there, and no good reason to change it. Hard to pack up and move on a whim with a bunch of baggage to bring along. That's why she always rented furnished houses or apartments.

"So where you from?"

Brady's pointed question yanked her back to his steady gaze. She licked her dry lips, almost unable to remember where she'd lived last. "New Jersey." Before that had been Chicago. No, Indianapolis.

Brady's eyebrows hitched higher on his forehead. "That's quite a ways. What brings you to Broken Bend?"

Brought her *back*. But no reason to dive into personal history best left buried. "My grandmother was put into the nursing home here. I was between jobs, so I thought I'd catch up with her." Redeem the past, as it were. If that was even possible at this point. Brady definitely didn't need to know she hadn't spoken to Nonie in years, and the woman had been deemed a ward of the state because Caley, her only living relative, had been unreachable for months. If her former church pastor hadn't seen the newspaper feature the *New York Times* had run on female firefighters from the South, Caley might still have no idea her grandmother needed her. The familiar wave of guilt pressed in thick and heavy like a scratchy wool blanket, and she cleared her throat.

Brady's eyes softened. "I'm sorry to hear that. I know the manager over there, and they run a great facility, if that helps you feel better about it."

The only thing that would make her feel better about the nursing home was if there wasn't a need for it at all. She'd hoped to be able to move Nonie into the rental house with her, but after talking to the staff on the phone and letting them know she was coming, she quickly realized home health care wasn't an option any of them could afford, nor could her grandmother's physical condition thrive without constant care. She'd have to redeem herself with daily visits—it was the least she could do for the woman who helped raise her.

"Who's your grandmother?"

She swallowed, determined not to let the wave of emotion overtake her. "Irene Foster." Her dad's mom, who'd never failed to try to explain her son to Caley, despite Caley's lack of interest in excuses. Motherly love might overlook a lot, but it was harder from a daughter's end of things. Not that it mattered much now. "I call her Nonie. She's a Broken Bend native."

"I recognize her name from the church prayer list. She's been on the homebound sheet for a while." Brady nodded, sympathy and something brighter—awareness?—lighting his eyes as his gaze held her own. "Well, neighbor, if you ever need help out here, just holler." He gave Ava a squeeze before he released her, then gently caught her chin and directed her gaze to his. "Though next time, little miss, you better ask permission before climbing over that fence. You hear?"

"Yes, sir." Ava ducked her head, her long hair draping over her flushed cheeks—but not before Caley caught the disappointment in her eyes. Disappointment over breaking a rule and being reprimanded? Or was it over not being able to visit and see Scooter freely?

Either way, she couldn't bear her crestfallen expression. "Ava is welcome here anytime—with your permission, of course. Scooter loves playmates." She caught her dog's collar with one hand and nudged him in the behind with her foot. He immediately sat and panted, his tongue lolling out the side of his mouth and giving the impression of a doggy smile.

"We'll see." Brady shuffled one boot against the driveway, the sole scraping against the rocky gravel. "She has plenty to keep her busy. I'm sure you don't need her underfoot over here."

Caley's stomach tightened. Was he trying to be polite and not impose? Or was this the brush-off? The attraction she'd felt toward Brady at first sight had definitely seemed reciprocated—however pointlessly. Still, why would he try to dodge her? Maybe he just wanted to make sure she really liked kids and Ava wasn't intruding. Besides, just because she couldn't embrace a relationship right now didn't mean she couldn't use a few friends—especially neighbors.

She straightened her shoulders and hoped her smile appeared more casual than it felt. "Ava would never be a problem here. In fact, I could use the company while I unpack." She turned to include Ava in the conversation instead of continuing to talk about her as if she wasn't there. "We might find some cookies somewhere in the truck. Want to help me look?"

"Yes! I mean—" Ava's eager eyes darted from Caley to her father and then back again, as if unsure if it was okay to answer honestly. "Dad? Can I?"

Brady scooped his hat off his head with one hand and ran his fingers through his rumpled hair. "I don't know, Ava."

Caley took advantage of his temporary hesitation. "It'd really help me out. I hate unpacking. And the quicker I get it done, the quicker I can get out and find a job." Especially now that her contact at the district fire station had proven slightly off in his assurance they would hire her. Turned out the guaranteed position wasn't as guaranteed as she'd hoped, and an upcoming budget meeting would determine her fate. Putting in some volunteer hours definitely wouldn't hurt the decision-making process, but she still had to find something to draw a paycheck in the interim.

Brady's expression tightened, as if just remembering bad news. "It's not that." He squinted down at Ava, shading his eyes from the sun peering over the roof's edge. "I came over here to find you because I just heard from Ms. Mary. Her sister broke her hip and she's got to go to Arkansas next week to help her out."

Concern furrowed the skin between Ava's eyebrows. "Is she going to be okay?"

"I think so, it just means Mary's going to be gone awhile. Several weeks, at best." He glanced at Caley. "Mary is Ava's nanny. She watches her after school and on the weekends while I'm out in the fields, and cooks and keeps up the house for me." He released a sigh heavy with burden. Caley could recognize that particular sound a mile away—it was an echo of her own. "So I'm sort of in the lurch right now."

Ava blinked up at her dad with childlike innocence. "But what does that have to do with me helping Caley?"

"*Miss* Caley," Brady corrected. He shook his head, a reluctant grin taking dominance over his shadowed expression. "And I guess not much. I'm the one stressing over figuring this out, not you."

"Then can I start right now?" Ava leaned down

and picked up the box of pillows and bird feeders from the ground, as if in effort to prove her work ethic.

"It really is okay. I can't eat those cookies alone, you know." Caley grinned, hooking one finger through Scooter's collar before he knocked over Ava and her box.

Brady pulled his cell phone from his back jeans pocket and checked the time. "Just until suppertime. You know Mary doesn't like us to be late for dinner." He replaced his phone and offered Caley a quick wink that not only surprised her, but automatically made her insides flutter with a swarm of line-dancing butterflies. "And I don't like cold potatoes."

Ha. So he wasn't all uptight, after all—just stressed over figuring out a new routine. She'd been there. Odd how she already had so much in common with her neighbors. Maybe her coming back to Broken Bend was for more than Nonie, after all. She'd have to be careful, though. She didn't do the commitment thing. But maybe she could somehow find a way to help this handsome cowboy and his adorable daughter and forget her own troubles for a while.

Temporarily, of course.

That new neighbor was going to be trouble. Brady could feel it in his bones. Just like his achy right knee meant it was going to rain later that night, he just knew he was going to eventually regret living next door to Caley Foster. Even if she was the prettiest thing he'd seen in a long time.

Or maybe *because* she was the prettiest thing he'd seen in a long time.

Brady swung easily over the fence separating his property from Caley's rental and strolled back to his horse, Nugget, grazing several yards away. Ava had taken to Caley quickly, and against his better judgment, so had he. And why wouldn't they? With those bright green eyes and charmingly messy blond hair—not to mention her grit and ability to take care of herself—Caley Foster seemed like a fresh breeze wafting through Broken Bend.

He just didn't have much room in his life for gusts of wind these days.

Still, there was something unique about a woman who moved cross-country by herself to take care of her grandmother in the nursing home—something that spoke of goodness and light. Something he didn't get much of these days, not with him and Ava constantly beating their heads like a couple of battering rams.

Nothing was the same anymore, and the new normal they'd created as a family of two instead of three felt awkward even at the best of times. A knot tightened in Brady's throat and he swallowed against it, though he knew the effort would be as wasted as trying to convince Ava she didn't belong on a workhorse beside him. A horse had killed her mom, and though everyone in town deemed it an accident, Brady knew better. It was his fault. He shouldn't have allowed Jessica on that high-strung beast in the first place, shouldn't have allowed her to insist she could handle it. Even though four years had passed, he couldn't erase the image of the stallion's flat ears and wide eyes before he reared up and threw Jessica off. Some memories were impossible to forget.

And some he was determined never to repeat. The farther away Ava stayed from the dangerous animals he worked around daily, the better off she was. She belonged in the house, where it was safe, with Mary. If he could, he'd up and move them somewhere else entirely, but Brady couldn't sell his livelihood. It ran through his blood. He had no way to make a living besides maintaining the land and animals that had been passed down to him from two generations before. The difference was, *he* knew what he was doing—a ten-year-old girl did not. He refused to allow anyone else he loved to be harmed.

Brady swung up on Nugget's back and nudged the horse toward the back forty acres, eyes automatically scanning the area for smoke. He'd gotten a little paranoid after the local fire department had issued a widespread warning about seasonal brush fires. The early-autumn winds and leftover summer temps could cause an issue in moments. Bad enough for any rancher—doubly bad for him, specifically.

He shook off the memories that threatened to lodge, reminding himself he wasn't a child anymore. He wasn't trying to prove himself on a daredevil prank, and he certainly wasn't trapped in a burning basement. He had plenty of issues to deal with now without being burdened by what wasn't real any longer—like Mary leaving, for example. He *must* be preoccupied to have left his daughter with a near stranger, but everything about Caley rang sincere and honest. Maybe it'd be good for Ava to make friends with a woman.

Besides, he'd told his daughter "no" so many times lately, Brady didn't think he could handle one more disappointed flash of her blue eyes.

He urged Nugget into a lope and rocked along with the familiar, comforting gait. He might be calloused from life, but he wasn't totally hardhearted.

Yet, anyway.

Chapter Two

"This box is marked *bath towels,* but it's full of Christmas ornaments." Ava held up a giant cup-cake ornament. The pink-and-green icing sparkled under the light from the dusty ceiling fan overhead as it twirled from her finger.

Caley propped her favorite—and only—painting against the living room wall and strode across the matted carpet to peer inside Ava's box. "You're right. I must have mixed them up last time I packed. So I guess the box marked *ornaments* is full of—"

"Dish towels?" Ava supplied.

Caley grinned, "I was going to guess silverware."

Ava snorted. "How often do you move, anyway?" She held a smaller box up for Caley to see how worn the bottom was. "Some of these boxes look…tired."

That was putting it nicely. "Pretty often. I like to travel, keep things interesting." More like keep from feeling too much, remembering. Regretting.

"That sounds like fun." Ava nestled the cupcake ornament back into the tissue paper, and folded the box shut. "We hardly ever leave the ranch. I know Dad would never move anywhere."

"What about vacations?" Caley found a box marked *cleaning supplies* and dug inside for a duster to clean the fan. She came up with a hammer instead, which she laid on the floor beside her beloved picture of a firefighter. She'd hang it later. "Do you and your dad ever take trips together?"

"We went to Dallas last year for a weekend, and he bought me some new shoes." Ava closed the ornament box and set it gently against the far wall, out of the way.

Dallas? That was maybe four hours away. Not much of a vacation—especially considering Brady could get Ava shoes at Walmart one county over. No wonder Ava and her dad seemed so strained. Did he ever take time away from the ranch to just hang out with her?

But it really wasn't Caley's business—however much she wanted to make it so. *Don't get involved. You're not going to be here long enough to make it count.* Story of her life. But it was safer that way. The fewer people whose lives she impacted personally, the better off they were. She'd stick to saving lives via the anonymity of the fire department. The emotional connections she'd leave up to someone else.

"I've been asking for a trip to Disney World for my birthday next year, but Dad says he can't leave the ranch for that long. Not even with Uncle Max here to help." Ava tossed a red throw pillow onto the worn blue love seat and shrugged as though it didn't matter.

But Caley knew from experience it did. Would things have been different between her and her own father growing up if he'd invested time in the little things after Mom left? Into the fun stuff that made memories? Instead, Caley grew up and had to go make her own memories alone. The first time she skydived, she'd been about ready to lose her breakfast inside the plane, but the thrill of the adventure to come pressed her forward. Why couldn't her father have ever taken the opportunity to be spontaneous? To trust? To *live?*

He couldn't do any of those things now, not from the Broken Bend graveyard twelve miles up the road. Regret rolled over in its familiar spot in her stomach. Her childhood might not have been ideal, but she still wished she had been given one more chance to redeem it.

Hopefully it wasn't too late for her and Nonie.

"You must really like firefighters." Ava lifted a decorative candle engraved with the Maltese cross from a box and wiggled it at Caley, shaking her from her negative track of thoughts. "First that giant picture, now this."

"That's because I am one." She winked and set the candle on a shelf built above the TV stand.

"Awesome." Ava stared at Caley with newfound respect.

She bit back a snort. Too bad adults weren't as easily impressed with female firefighters.

Ava continued with her awestruck gaze. "Do you really put fires out and everything?"

"Yes, and help people who are hurt." She took the lid off a flat storage bin and grinned at Ava. "Hey, I found the silverware."

Ava scooted over to her and rummaged through the box. "And your alarm clock." She giggled.

"Next move, I'll be better organized." Definitely couldn't be worse. She hefted the box onto her hip and moved into the open kitchen to begin loading the drawers. "Why don't you go plug the clock into the outlet by the mattress?" She didn't own an actual bed; it was too complicated since she moved so often. A mattress on the floor with a pile of her grandmother's old-fashioned quilts worked just as well, and the early memories those blankets stirred up kept her warmer than any down comforter could.

"You should definitely get more organized, but I hope you don't move again soon." Ava hesitated in the doorway separating Caley's bedroom from the living room. She ducked her head a little, the expression in her eyes cautious, yet sincere. "You're really fun." She offered a slight smile before disappearing around the corner with the clock.

Caley's hands stilled on the pile of silverware she'd been separating into the divider. She didn't know how long she'd have to stay in Broken Bend, but it wouldn't do anyone any good to get attached. Still, something about Ava drew her like a magnet—or maybe more like a mama duck to a duckling. She'd read enough self-help books over the years, though, to know that butting into Ava's life in some pathetic effort to make up for her own childhood wouldn't accomplish anything.

And as for Ava's dad—well, Caley couldn't think about that particular connection. Mama duckling was one thing, but the attraction she'd felt at first sight for Brady McCollough was certainly nothing to pursue. She'd do everyone a favor if she kept to herself and stayed as invisible as possible while she did her time in Broken Bend. Soon enough she'd be somewhere else, a distant memory of a fun neighbor Ava once had. Maybe she could leave some good behind her before she went.

But she was definitely going.

"Look what I found! Kitchen towels!" Ava rushed into the kitchen with a box labeled *dishes* in bold marker and grinned.

"Good job, detective. They can go in here." Caley laughed as she pulled open a drawer, and Ava began filling it with the assortment of mismatched rags.

The younger girl paused and squinted, lips twitched to one side. "So do you think the box marked *dishes* will have bathroom towels in it?"

"You know what?" Caley shut the silverware drawer with her hip and wrapped one arm around Ava, joy filling her heart despite her earlier reservations. She squeezed Ava tight and grinned, determined not to let the inevitable spoil the moment. "I think you're catching on."

Brady knocked on Caley's front door, then stepped back while he waited. Scooter pranced at his feet, shamelessly begging for a treat. Caley must have left him outside while they unpacked. From the holes the dog had already dug in the poor excuse for a flowerbed by the porch, that had probably been a good idea.

Loud laughter suddenly rang from inside the house, followed by a blast of country music. Brady frowned and knocked again. Mary would have supper ready any minute, and after the afternoon he had spent on the phone, scrambling to find a temporary babysitter, he was ready to sit, eat—and pray for mercy.

The door swung open, offering a rush of boot-scootin' lyrics and Ava's wide white grin. But her face morphed into panic as their eyes locked. "Dad! I was going to come home on time, I promise." She looked at her wrist, but must have forgotten her watch, because her arm was bare. She rubbed the spot it should have rested and turned pleading eyes to him.

The anxiety in her expression chafed Brady's heart, and he cleared his throat. He knew they hadn't been exactly close lately, but was she actually afraid of making him mad over little things now? He would have never given himself a Dad of the Year award, but this realization stung. When had he gotten so bad?

"Don't worry, you're not in trouble." He plucked a dust bunny off Ava's shirtsleeve and wiped it on his jeans. "Looks like you've been working hard."

"We both have. It was fun—like a treasure hunt." Ava's face lit back up as though he'd plugged it in, and jealousy sparked in his stomach. His daughter had more fun with a near stranger in two hours' time than she did with him. Though he couldn't remember the last time he'd spent two hours in a row doing something with her other than chores—or fussing.

Ava slipped outside, half shutting the door to block the music from within. "And Caley has this really funny way of labeling boxes. You wouldn't believe—"

Brady interrupted. "*Miss* Caley. She's an adult."

"Yes, sir." Ava's shoulders slumped, light extinguished. "I won't forget again. Sorry."

"It's not—" Brady rubbed his fingers down his cheeks, frustration rising inside. He wanted to tell her not to apologize, not to think of him as an ogre, but he couldn't find the words. So he dropped his hands to his sides and shrugged. "Listen, I'm sure you've done a great job for Miss Caley. I just wanted to walk you home, since it's getting dark now. Supper's ready."

Ava nodded, though she still didn't light up like she had before. Was the thought of going home that disappointing? His throat tightened into a knot. "Let me just tell Caley—I mean, Miss Caley—that I'm leaving."

Brady stepped over the threshold, following Ava inside the house, and turned the corner of the short entranceway in time to see Caley standing on a dining room chair, dusting the ceiling fan with a feathery contraption on a stick. She swung her hips in time to the music still blaring from what had to be the world's oldest stereo, perched on the dining table by the kitchen door. Brady couldn't help the grin sliding across his face, and he leaned against the door frame, content to watch. Maybe supper *could* wait for some things.

"Miss Caley?" Ava cupped her hands around her mouth and yelled louder. "Miss Caley!"

Caley turned around with a jerk, balancing herself by catching a fan blade in one hand. Her eyes landed on Brady, and she flushed. "Oh, hey." She grinned, cheeks flaming as Ava ran to turn down the music. "Um, I found the duster." She wielded it as proof, whatever that thing was. Good thing Mary took care of the cleaning around the ranch house, though Brady had certainly never seen her do *that*.

He ambled upright and crossed his arms over his chest. "I see you've both been busy." And had probably accomplished a lot more than he had, running into dead end after dead end in the babysitting department. The teens that his church secretary recommended were too young for his comfort level, and the older ladies had too many stipulations and couldn't conform to his needed schedule. Looked as though he'd be calling an agency next—but what were the odds that residents of a small town like Broken Bend signed up for those organized programs? Would a nanny be willing to commute to town almost every day?

Caley hopped down from the chair, breaking his stressful chain of thought, and Brady mentally kicked himself for not having offered his hand to help her. Everything about Caley seemed so confident and capable, though, that it took him off guard. His wife had definitely been the opposite.

"We've gotten a lot done, though it still looks

like a wreck." She grinned. "I'm used to it, though. It always takes making a bigger mess before you get it clean."

No doubt about that. His life could be a prime example. But he wasn't interested in sorting through the rubble. He'd done that for years without seeing results—positive ones, anyway. He sat through church these days for Ava's sake, and Ava's sake alone. She needed the foundation, but his had long since crumbled.

Brady cleared his throat. "Ava and I need to get home for supper. It's going to be the last decent one we have for a while." Oops. He hadn't meant to let that slip. He must be more tired than he thought.

Ava's eyes narrowed with suspicion—probably because she knew he couldn't boil a pot of water to save anyone's life. "No luck finding me a sitter?"

"Not yet." He ran a hand over his jaw, the stubble whisking across his palm. "I'm going to have to—"

"What about Caley?" The sparkle in Ava's eyes burst into a roaring flame of hope as she brought both hands up to her chin in a pleading position. "I mean, Miss Caley."

"Me?" Caley pulled slightly away from Ava to look at her more directly, overly dramatized shock radiating from her eyes. "Babysit? *You?*"

Ava's face fell. "Is it that bad of an idea?"

Yes. Brady opened his mouth to speak the truth, to tell Ava that there was no way Caley needed to come over to their house—his domain—and take care of them. Feed them. Clean up after them.

Invade his territory with her cinnamon scent and uncanny ability to stir feelings long dormant.

"I'm kidding!" Caley laughed and hip-bumped Ava, who bounced off her side, giggling. "I think it's a perfect idea!" Then she sobered. "As long as your dad thinks so, of course." As if on cue, both of them linked arms and turned doe eyes on him.

Perfect idea? More like the worst. He needed a kind older woman who was in agreement with his firm rules for Ava—not a hip young woman who acted more like Ava's older sister than an adult. Ava didn't need fun right now. She needed structure. Security.

Safety.

So did he. One look at the playful pout turning down Caley's full lips, and safe was the last thing Brady felt. Something about Caley seemed way too dangerous. Not in an ax-murderer-next-door kind of way, but in a she's-gonna-weasel-into-your-heart kind of way. He hadn't thought much about romance since Jessica's death—who had the time between the frequent guilt trips and running a ranch?—but Caley's teasing eyes and trim figure coaxed to life embers he'd thought long dead. Being around her any more than necessary seemed incredibly risky.

And he didn't take risks.

"It's not just babysitting, Ava. It's cooking and housekeeping, too."

Caley shrugged. "I'm still in."

He started shaking his head, mind racing through the implications of letting Caley that close, until Ava piped up once again. "Dad, who else is there to hire at the last minute? Miss Caley just said today that she needed to find a job soon. This works for everyone!"

It did, didn't it? How did one argue against such youthful logic? Brady began to wish he'd just stayed outside with Scooter instead of being ganged up on by two insistent females. But maybe the idea was a decent one. He'd be outside most of the time, anyway, and Ava and Caley already had an evident bond. He'd just been thinking that it'd be good for Ava to have a womanly influence. Just because Caley wasn't blue-haired and bifocaled didn't mean she couldn't be a positive role model. She was here to take care of her sick grandma, after all. And she was obviously capable.

"I do need the work, and with it being temporary, it seems ideal." Caley's curved eyebrows rose with prompting. "I have nanny experience from college, and I'm a licensed EMT."

Well, he wouldn't find better credentials than that through the church.

His gaze darted to his daughter, whose pleading expression froze the rest of his resistance. He couldn't tell her no again. If spending time with Caley made Ava happy, he'd find a way to survive the next few weeks. How hard could it be? At least he'd get a hot meal without having to order pizza every night for the next month. And who knew—maybe he and Caley could be friends.

Just friends.

"Okay, you've convinced me." Brady held up both hands to fend off Ava's excited squeal as she jumped up and down. "Caley, you can start Monday. Ava is out from school the first half of next week for teacher conferences, so she can show you the ropes at the house. And to be fair, I'll pay you what I was paying Mary." He named the figure, and Caley nodded with approval.

"I'd have done it for less." She winked, and Ava laughed out loud. Brady bit back a groan. He was in trouble, all right. Trouble with a capital *C*.

Yet as he caught the two blondes' excited high five, he decided trouble couldn't come in a cuter package.

Chapter Three

Caley really hoped she didn't regret this.

She stared up at the beautiful, sprawling Double C ranch house and paused before knocking on the solid oak door. Birds chirped a welcoming chorus she wasn't certain Brady would agree with. His hesitation at hiring her had caught her off guard. Was it just because she was a near stranger? If he was worried about that, though, he wouldn't have let Ava help her unpack for a few hours. So if not safety or trust, then was it her ability? Maybe he doubted her capability in the house. Well, she'd show him. She might not be a gourmet chef, but she'd learned some good recipes over the years of her life on the go, and she obviously knew how to wield a duster.

She straightened her spine and knocked. For her first day, she'd whip up Nonie's secret-ingredient chocolate chip cookies. That'd show him.

But why she felt such a strong urge to prove herself to Brady—impress him, even, if she was honest—she couldn't say.

The door flew open, and Ava's beaming smile swept away Caley's insecurities. She wasn't here for Brady, cookies or not, approval or not. She was here for this sweet little girl who needed quality care and a positive female influence in her life. As long as she remembered that, they'd be just fine. She'd get a paycheck while waiting to hear about a job from the fire department, and Ava would get plenty of girl time.

Brady would probably just get a headache, but that was his own fault.

"Come on in!" Ava practically squealed as she grabbed Caley's arm and pulled her through the doorway. "I cleaned my room. Dad told me I had to. I think he didn't want to scare you off before you even started."

She giggled, and the enthusiasm in her expression made Caley almost want to go back and agree to babysit for free, after all. But she enjoyed electricity and food.

"Sounds good. Let's go see it." She squeezed Ava's hand and followed the girl toward the straight staircase leading up to the second floor. On her way, she cast a quick glance over the nearly suffocatingly pristine living room. Full bookshelves surrounded the TV on both sides, the top shelves reserved for an obviously cherished collection of bronze horse and cowboy statues. The furniture, while not new by any means, seemed as if it'd been kept up neatly. Caley made a mental note—no snacking in the living room. A worn but clean rug covered the hardwood floor under a dark-chocolate-colored coffee table, yet hardly any art decorated the walls besides a lone school picture over a side table near the front door. Talk about a man's domain.

A neat-freak man, at that.

Ava's room was a different story. In fact, Caley would have loved to have seen it before she cleaned it. It would've been like viewing a train wreck. Trash spilled from the overflowing purple wastebasket beside a short desk probably meant for homework, but covered in the remnants of an abandoned art project. Novels and textbooks on horses and farm animals were stacked haphazardly beside—not on—the short purple bookshelf, and a herd of stuffed animals grazed at all angles atop the wrinkled, crooked, purple-and-green floral bedspread. Toys peeked from beneath the bed, and a jumble of puzzle pieces had been shoved under the desk. Every drawer on the dresser was partially open with clothes hanging out.

While the room definitely needed more attention, Caley couldn't help but smile at the ways Ava and her father were so drastically different—and yet cringe at the myriad ways this would inevitably cause more problems between the two of them. Maybe she could somehow help Ava find a balance between being herself and pleasing her father.

"What do you think?" Ava spun a slow circle in the center of her room, eyes narrowed critically. "Dad said he'd hang those glow-in-the-dark stars above my bed soon, but he hasn't yet."

"I think that would be awesome." Caley moved to perch on the edge of the bed and looked up. "They'd be perfect right there." She pointed.

"I concur." Brady's deep voice broke the silence as he peered around the door frame at them, his dark hair falling across his forehead without the presence of his cowboy hat. Caley ignored the tingles in her stomach. "But I told Ava she had to keep her room clean enough to *see* the ceiling first."

"Da-*ad*." Ava's tone stretched the word into several syllables, tinted with embarrassment. "It's not that bad. See?" She gestured around the room, and Caley suddenly realized the closet door actually bulged a little.

"It's been worse." Brady crossed his arms across the front of his plaid work shirt, muscles cording beneath the rolled-up sleeves. "But it's been better. I don't want you to put this off on Miss Caley. She's here to clean for us, but that's just basic upkeep." His penetrating gaze registered on her, drawing her in despite her initial reserve. "I don't expect you to clean to this degree." An unfamiliar twinkle slowly lit his expression. "I don't think a landfill worker could be expected to clean to this degree."

"I don't mind." The words slipped from her lips before she could edit them, and she told herself it was just because of her desire to see Ava and her dad get along—and not based on any desire to make him happy personally. Caley shook her head. What was wrong with her? She'd better curb this one-sided attraction now. Brady was essentially her boss—at least until the fire department let her know what was going on. She still needed to put in some volunteer hours—not to mention spend time with her grandmother, the sole reason she was back in this town in the first place. Somehow, she'd work it all in. She had to keep her eye on the greater goals—future employment with the fire department and quality time with her blood family.

Regardless of the immediate future, this arrangement with Brady—no, Ava—was most definitely temporary.

She forced a smile, hoping it didn't look as fake as it felt, as she stood up from the bed. "It'll be fine. Ava and I can make it into a project." She'd need to borrow a wheelbarrow. And that big green tractor she saw parked outside earlier. But she liked taking risks. She cast another glance at the closet door. Big risks. "What do you say, Ava?"

Ava shrugged good-naturedly. "Whatever it takes to get my stars. Besides, it'd be much more fun to do it with you than with—" Her voice trailed off as she shot a glance at her father and looked quickly away, red tinting her cheeks.

Brady's gaze darted to the ground, then back up, his Adam's apple bobbing in his throat. "I just came in to say hi and welcome." He nodded, all hint of his former teasing gone from his eyes. "If you need anything, Ava can help you find it, or you can holler at me later. I'll be in for dinner at six-thirty."

He was gone from sight before he even finished speaking the words, yet the hurt in his tone lingered long after.

Caley waited, wondering if Ava would address the new elephant in the room, but the young girl simply pressed her lips together into a tight line and released a sigh through her nose. She clearly hadn't meant to hurt her dad's feelings, but as Caley well knew, sometimes honesty drove a sharp knife. Hopefully Brady wouldn't take it personally. What ten-year-old girl wouldn't rather clean her room with her new babysitter than with her rule-bearing father?

Somehow, though, the tension in the room suggested a lot more behind the scenes than that.

"Time to clean, huh?" Ava's dismal voice suggested she'd rather go muck out the stalls in the barn—and judging from their past conversations, she'd literally prefer it. But her dad wouldn't allow her to venture toward the animals. Did they agree on anything?

Caley gathered her inner resolve. She'd do whatever she could to make this fun for them both. She nodded, shoving her hands in her back pockets and feigning a grave expression. "I believe so. Why don't you show me where the trash bags are?" She waited until Ava caught her eye, then she winked. "And I'll find the chocolate."

The smile now back on Ava's face was more than worth the overwhelming task before them.

Brady couldn't decide if he was more coated in dust or annoyance.

"I caught him." His longtime best friend and only hired hand, Max Ringgold, looped Nugget's reins around the hitching post outside the barn, then slapped at the dirt clinging to Brady's shirtsleeves and back. "He came barreling through here like a Thoroughbred. I'd have been worried if I hadn't seen you hobbling after him a minute later." Max's brow pinched in mock concern. "Didn't anyone ever tell you to take shelter during a dust storm?"

"Funny." Brady stepped away from the good-natured beating his friend doled out. "I'll remember that next time." As if he'd had a lot of choices out in the middle of the pasture, without a horse or even a saddle blanket to toss over his head. It figured that he left his bandanna in the house today of all days.

"Too bad you weren't in the barn like I was when it blew through." Max's smile broadened. He was clearly finding way too much humor in his boss's appearance.

Brady squinted off at the now calm pastures, then aimed a pointed look at his friend. "Too bad someone didn't warn their boss."

"What, you think I'm in the barn watching the Weather Channel?" Max adjusted the black hat on his head, still grinning. "That dust storm spiraled up in the fields from nowhere and left just as quickly."

Max was right. It'd been unavoidable. All part of the unknowns of working a ranch—and another reason that just confirmed his instincts to keep Ava in the house, where it was safe. Away from unpredictable weather and brush fires and even more unpredictable animals—like Nugget, who had thrown him off at the first ruffle of wind. Blasted creature had gone running to the safety of the barn—leaving Brady to walk after him, gritting dirt between his teeth.

"I'm surprised you're getting anything done out

here anyway, with the new nanny inside." Max winked. "I'm sure she's capable, but may I say, she's a far cry from Ms. Mary."

A sprig of jealousy burst into full bloom. He knew his friend was just teasing, but for some reason, it rubbed him wrong. He forced a smile to look friendly, but his tone was all boss. "The new nanny is off-limits." For both of them. For multiple reasons.

But especially for Max.

Max sidestepped as Nugget reached over to nibble the grass near his boots. "You know me, man. I'm just a sucker for a pretty face. I don't act on it."

Brady snorted. "You have before." He ticked off names on his finger. "Brenda. Lucy. Michelle."

Max shook his head, hands up in surrender. "They weren't fellow employees." He shaded his eyes against the sun and looked over at the main house, as if trying to get a glimpse inside. "She's just temporary, though, right?"

Brady's jaw tightened and Max laughed. "I'm kidding, boss. Sorry, I guess I wouldn't be in a joking mood if I looked like you, either." He gave Brady's shoulder another hearty pat, and more dirt puffed from his sleeve. "Go get cleaned up. I'll take care of the dust bunny here." He gestured to Nugget.

"You might want to brush off his tack, too." Brady strode toward the house, his tone leaving no question about who was in charge. He loved Max like a brother, but sometimes he wondered if hiring his best friend was a smart move. Too often they blurred the line between respect and fun, and Brady had a hard time sharpening it back into focus. He had to admit, though, if Max had been teasing about any other girl from church or town, he couldn't have cared less. Something about Caley was different, and that made him as skittish as Nugget had been in the storm.

Hopefully things were going better in the house than they had been for him outside. The girls wouldn't be expecting him until later this evening for supper, but he couldn't keep doing his chores for the remainder of the afternoon until he brushed his teeth and changed shirts.

Brady strode into the house, the back door banging shut behind him harder than he meant to let it. Ava and Caley looked up with a start from the kitchen counter, where a mass of something that might be cookie dough clung to a greased sheet in tiny, uneven mounds. Ava had flour smeared on her cheeks, and a speckle of dough clung to the apron Caley had donned over her top and jeans. They both looked at him, then at their own mess, and laughed.

"I didn't know it was flouring outside, too." Caley clapped her hands together and a puff of white powder flurried into the air.

Brady couldn't stay frustrated about his current condition, or even Max—not with the three of them looking the way they all did. He cracked a smile and brushed at his jeans. Dirt showered onto the floor. "Something like that."

"Hey, Caley just swept that." Ava's indignant defense lost its merit when she was covered in flour. She handed her dad the broom leaning against the kitchen wall.

Caley snatched it back before Brady could figure out how to get to his room to change without tracking more dirt everywhere. "No worries. We should have waited until after the cookies were done, anyway. This was a bigger mess than I thought."

"Those are cookies?" Brady raised an eyebrow. Who'd have thought? His stomach rumbled with protest. It might turn out that Mary and Caley were opposites in more ways than he'd expected.

Caley snorted. "Supposed to be. We'll see when they get out of the oven. It's a recipe my grandmother made for me my entire childhood, but…I think I forgot something." She poked at one of the mounds with a spoon—it didn't budge. She wrinkled her nose. "Or maybe we just should start over."

"I think I'll take a dirt storm over a flour storm any day." Brady shook his head with a smile. Funny how just being around Caley brightened his mood. He and Max were going to be in more trouble than he originally thought. "I'm going to go change." And hopefully remind himself while he was gone of all the reasons why he couldn't think of the woman slinging dough in his kitchen as anything other than a temporary employee.

"You don't want to stay and help?" Ava's hopeful expression cast a shadow on his brightening mood. Brady sighed. Here he went, about to disappoint his daughter once again. He hated keeping score, but he couldn't help but feel as if the board would read Brady: 0, Caley: 2. Or was she up to 3 by now? Either way, he was far behind in the game of good graces. He still smarted from Ava's comment in her room earlier that morning.

But the ranch wouldn't run itself, and Ava should be old enough to understand that by now. If he stayed in the kitchen and made cookies all afternoon, who would feed the animals? Who would fix the broken barbed-wire fence in the south pasture? Who would clean the rest of the stalls he'd started that morning and check on the pregnant mare? Not to mention the stack of invoices he needed to mail for the hay he'd sold last week. Max helped out, but the ranch was more than enough work for two men.

In fact, if he thought about it long enough, he'd go insane from the pressure. He was stuck and couldn't please everyone. He *had* to support them, and as much as he'd like to play with Ava all day, he just couldn't. That's what Mary was for—and now, Caley. One day, he'd get caught up and be more available. One day.

Brady stepped gingerly toward the kitchen door leading into the living room, aware of his dusty tracks. "I'm sorry, honey. I've got a lot more to do outside. That storm just caught me off guard, is all. Need to change and get back to it." He tried to overlook Ava's crestfallen expression and Caley's pursed lips, and lifted his tone in an effort to lighten the suddenly somber mood. "I'll see you for supper, though."

They ignored him, except for Ava's bottom lip poking farther out.

He attempted a joke. "Hopefully supper turns out better than those cookies."

Two sets of eyes simultaneously flicked his direction and narrowed. Not the time for humor, obviously.

"If you can't stay in here, then can I come help you outside?" Ava's timid voice held zero hope, as if she already knew the answer. And she did.

Brady shook his head slowly. "You know the rules. Your chores are in the house, not with the animals. It's too dangerous."

"But, Dad—" Ava broke off as Caley nudged her in the side. She sighed. "Yes, sir."

He was proud of her for remembering her

manners, but couldn't find the words to say so. It wouldn't matter, anyway. That wasn't what she wanted to hear. Brady slipped upstairs without another comment, wondering how on earth he'd even be able to eat dinner that night with the solid rock of guilt taking up his entire stomach.

He wrenched his dirty clothes into the hamper and changed into a fresh shirt, then brushed his teeth with more aggression than necessary. He wasn't sure what was more unsettlingly, the fact that he couldn't seem to do anything right in his daughter's eyes…

Or how much he'd enjoyed seeing Caley in his kitchen after a long day of work.

Chapter Four

She'd missed the smell of the bay.

Caley breathed in the familiar scent of motor oil, exhaust and lemon cleaner. It must have been a bay day on the chores schedule, by the looks of the squeaky-clean concrete beneath her boots. She didn't particularly miss pushing a mop over the floor or scrubbing down trucks, but she missed the activity. The excitement. The adrenaline rush that flowed through her veins with the knowledge that any minute, the alarm could chime and they'd be off to save lives.

Hopefully the job at the Broken Bend Fire Department would eventually work out. Because as fun as it'd been babysitting Ava that day, Caley's heart remained in the action of firefighting. Saving lives. Making a difference.

Making atonement.

Muffled voices and a sharp tapping sounded

from the far corner, where a group of blue-uniformed firemen stocked the back of the ambulance. She hated to interrupt if they were counting supplies, but she needed to find Captain O'Donnell to ask about her volunteer gear. If she was going to start doing ride-outs and earning her way into the station, she needed to get set up ASAP.

Caley lifted one hand in a wave to the older man who broke from the group and strode toward her with a curious expression. There was the captain now, judging by the embroidery on his blue polo. "Good evenin'. Can we help you, ma'am?"

The other firemen glanced up with interest, but went back to their stocking after a firm glance from the captain. She held out her hand. "I'm Caley Foster. I've come for my volunteer pager and gear."

The gray-bearded man offered a friendly smile and a firm handshake. "That's right. Chief Talbot said you'd be by this week. Come on in." He led the way past the recently washed fire trucks and held the station door open for her. "Nice to meet you."

Caley smiled her thanks, taking an appreciative note of his sincerity. As a female firefighter, she'd been treated in numerous ways over the years—dealing with everything from jealousy to discrimination to sexual harassment. The captain's respectful handshake and the way he met her eyes when he talked showed he considered her a capable equal, while his opening the door for her proved he was a gentleman at heart. Exactly the kind of captain she'd like to work for.

Captain picked up a pager from the cluttered desk to the right of the kitchen area, pressed a button and then nodded with satisfaction at the responding beep. "You're all set." He handed it to her, along with a BBFD T-shirt and a sheaf of paperwork. "Just sign these forms and we'll get them filed. I'm sure you've seen them before, based on Chief's report. This ain't your first rodeo, is it?" He winked beneath silver eyebrows, thicker than his beard.

She liked Captain. "You could say that." Caley grabbed a pen from the coffee mug on the corner, took a seat at the table and began scribbling her signature in the designated areas. "What about bunker gear?"

"We have extra sets up here that stay in the bay lockers. You're welcome to those whenever you come meet the trucks." Captain shrugged, leaning forward to brace his arms on the chair across from her. "Or just swing by and grab them before you meet us in the field. Either way. We've had issues in the past about volunteers not returning their gear after quitting, so Chief decided that volunteer gear should stay on-site."

"Understandable." Caley scribbled her name on

the last document and stacked them neatly before handing them over to Captain. "I'm renting a place only about fifteen miles from here, so I can make it pretty quick in an emergency."

Captain glanced at the address that had already been typed into her paperwork. "That's next door to the Double C ranch, isn't it? McCollough's place."

"You know him?"

"Everyone knows McCollough, after the tragedy he went through few years back. He's a good ol' boy." Captain slid Caley's paperwork inside a green folder. "I see him at church from time to time. He and that kid of his—they've had some tough breaks."

"I'm actually babysitting his daughter for now. They had an emergency come up with their nanny—temporarily, of course." Caley held up both hands in an effort to clarify and grinned. "I'm sure you know I'm hoping to get hired on here."

"We'd love to have you. It's rare getting a volunteer with as much experience as you've had." Captain shrugged, shoving his hands into his pants pockets. "Not my call, but you'd have my vote if it was."

"I appreciate it." Caley hesitated, grateful for the confidence Captain had in her, but unsure how to far to push. Still, something he said lingered on the fringes of her brain and demanded details.

"You mentioned how Brady and Ava have been through a lot—what exactly happened with Ava's mom?" She held her breath, hoping a few pieces of the puzzle that was all things Brady McCollough would finally slide into place. She hated to seem nosy, but no one was volunteering the information, and if she wanted to make a difference—for Ava's sake, of course—then it could only help her to know what they'd overcome.

Or rather, what they were still attempting to overcome.

"It was an accident." Captain looked toward the bay with a heavy sigh, and Caley suddenly felt as if she was being dismissed. "But that's a story for McCollough to tell."

"I see. Well, thank you. I won't keep you." She quickly stood and held out her hand for a goodbye shake, mentally kicking herself for coming across as a gossiping, meddling newcomer. She might be a born-and-bred native of Broken Bend, but she'd been gone so long she'd likely crossed the line from family to foreigner long ago. "Thanks for getting me set up. You'll definitely be seeing me around." First time that pager buzzed, she'd be on it.

That is, if she wasn't on babysitting duty. Caley rolled in her lower lip. Balancing her time between making volunteer runs, visiting Nonie and watching Ava might not be as easy as she'd thought.

"I hope so, Ms. Foster." Captain motioned her to walk out the bay door ahead of him. "And a word to the wise—if you truly want to get hired on here, don't just show up for the fun stuff."

Meaning fires. "Got it. Thanks for the tip. I'll be well-rounded, I promise." She crossed the bay toward her car, T-shirt tucked under her arm.

"Ms. Foster?"

She turned at the sound of Captain's deep voice and arched an eyebrow, waiting for more inside advice. "Yes, sir?"

"If I were you, I'd not press McCollough. It's not a story he likes to tell."

Brady adjusted the pillow under his head, shifting onto his side as he waited for sleep to come. But for the first time in months, he found himself wide-awake at the end of the day. It certainly wasn't due to lack of hard work—after the dust storm, he'd gone right back to it, despite the sullen glances Ava shot his way. No, he had a feeling his inability to sleep had a lot more to do with the feisty little woman who'd botched not only two but three dozen cookies. Whatever secret recipe her Nonie used to make was apparently destined to remain a secret.

Brady flipped onto his back and sighed, unable to erase the mental image of Caley with flour smeared on her cheeks and dotting her forearms, winking as she managed to accomplish the one thing he never could with Ava these days—making her smile.

And she'd be back in his kitchen doing it all again the next day.

The realization brought equal parts joy and panic. Dismissing the idea of sleep, Brady threw on a pair of Wranglers and a T-shirt, slid into his boots and quietly slipped outside. Maybe fresh air and a quick walk would clear his head, remind him of all the reasons why even though it felt right having Caley in his home, it was wrong.

He'd failed at being a husband once and was making pretty good time on messing up fatherhood, too. He didn't dare bring another woman into his life—even if Caley was sweet. Wholesome. Sincere. She baked cookies and took care of her grandmother in the nursing home. She was the very picture of a rancher's wife. Good with his daughter. Smiled a lot.

Would probably look cute in boots.

The night breeze stirred Brady's hair, and he wished he'd brought his hat. He realized with a jolt that he'd headed toward Caley's property, and now a soft glow from her back window lit the night like a beacon. He slowed his pace, unsure why he'd come that way and berating his subconscious for being a traitor. He started to turn around, not trusting himself to walk any closer. Something about

Caley called to him, and if he ever answered, it'd be catastrophic for them all.

"I found the Little Dipper."

Brady nearly stumbled over a gopher hole as Caley's gentle voice broke the silence of the night. "What? Where?" He looked around to find the person attached to the voice but saw no one. Had he officially lost it? He knew hiring Caley had been a bad idea. Now he was conjuring her voice out of the prairie.

A muffled giggle sounded from above. "Up here."

He drew his gaze to the sound. The roof. She waved from her reclined position on a blanket, sprawled out directly under the stars. A wiggling black blob he could only assume was Scooter lay nestled on the quilt by her side. "Caley? What are you doing up there?" He felt the urge to cup his hand over his eyes as he looked up, despite the sun not being out. How on earth did she get that dog up there?

She rose to a sitting position, hair tousled, making her look all the cuter. "Come on up. The view is great."

Brady shook his head. She must be crazy. Ava was home in bed, and he needed to get back to the house. Not to mention that he didn't love heights in the first place, and that ladder looked as if it was possibly older than the rental house.

Then she reached over and patted the shingles beside her in invitation, and he'd scaled three rungs before he even realized he was moving.

Drawing a breath, Brady settled a respectful distance away on the other side of the blanket and pulled his knees up to his chest for balance. "Sort of dangerous up here, isn't it?" He didn't look down, but focused on Caley's eyes glittering in the moonlight. Talk about dangerous.

She absently ran a hand over Scooter's back, smoothing his fur. "You sound like my dad."

Definitely not his intention. Brady cleared his throat, unsure how to backpedal. "I just didn't expect to see you up here, that's all." Women he knew didn't sit on roofs. Then again, he didn't know a whole lot of women anymore. Didn't seem fair to compare everyone to Jessica, but that's all he had to go on. Not for the first time, he wished he'd let his play-it-safe wife stay that way. Instead, he'd been so taken aback by her request to ride that he'd eagerly agreed, despite knowing better. She'd finally shown some effort toward his interests—toward their marriage—and he wasn't about to curb it.

And look what happened.

Brady scooted a little farther away from the edge of the roof, wishing Caley would do the same. Instead, she tilted her head back as she studied the sky, her short blond hair skimming down her back.

"The view is great." She gestured to the heavens. "It was one of the things I'd missed about country life."

He felt himself being pulled in, like a moth to a lit candle. Against his will. Fascinated. Yet destined to get burned. "What else did you miss?"

She pulled in her lower lip, and took her time answering. "Peace and quiet. And space. Living in big cities is exciting, but it's constant noise, constant action. Like there's always something else you should be doing." She lifted one shoulder in a shrug. "It gets exhausting."

"I can only imagine." He'd only ever known ranch life, and that was fine with him. Cities had too much concrete. A man needed earth under his boots, not man-made rock. "So why'd you move to a city?"

She sucked in a hard breath, and repositioned her jeans-clad legs underneath her. "Long story." She offered a sideways smile, and he forced himself to hold her gaze despite the magnetism tipping him off balance. "I'm here for Nonie now, and that's all that matters."

Closed door on that topic. Probably for the best. He didn't need to carry her secrets, even if some deep-rooted part of him wanted to. "Have you seen your grandmother yet?" Brady plucked a leaf from the shingles beside him and began to shred it, eager for something to do with his hands before he shoved another proverbial foot in his mouth.

"Not yet. I spent the weekend getting settled and hitting the grocery store." She exhaled slowly, turning her eyes back to the inky sky. "I was going to go tomorrow after work." Her voice trailed off, as if she'd almost forgotten he was there. "I need to, anyway."

"You could take Ava, if you wanted." The words flew out before he could process them, but the idea made sense—not to mention it seemed to combat the anxiety in her expression. It didn't make sense. If she moved to Broken Bend to take care of her beloved grandmother, then why hadn't she run over there the moment she crossed the county line?

Maybe that was part of the secret she carried.

"You wouldn't mind?" Hope filled the hollow spots in her voice, and Brady suddenly hoped she didn't ask him to rope the moon. Because in that moment, he'd have gladly headed out to the barn for his lasso.

His leaf was gone, shredded to pieces in his lap. He brushed off his jeans. "Not at all. It'd be good for her. And speaking of Ava, I need to get back in case she wakes up and finds me gone."

Caley stood as he did, and he offered his hand for assistance. She either ignored it or didn't see it, because she nimbly turned backward and scurried halfway down the ladder like a squirrel on tree bark. She clapped her hands twice, and Scooter obediently came to the edge of the rungs. She reached up for him, tucked him against her side and climbed down a few more feet until she could safely drop him to the grass.

That was something he didn't see every day. Brady followed at a slower pace, not breathing regularly until her feet were on solid ground—and all too aware that the dog was less afraid of heights than he.

"Does she usually wake up in the middle of the night?" Caley tucked her hair behind her ears, eyes full of compassion.

He centered himself back on earth before he answered. "Not usually, but in the last few years since her mom's death, she gets the occasional nightmare." More like night terror, the way Ava woke up, crying and pounding on his bedroom door. She hadn't had one in months.

"Has she seen a counselor about it?" Caley turned, the moonshine turning her hair nearly white.

"She saw one in the year after, and the counselor assured me her grief was typical and would go through stages." Brady ran his hand over his own hair, really wishing for his hat now. Anything to try to guard himself from Caley's inquisitive stare. Her eyes darted between his, and he could almost see the wheels turning. "She's fine, I promise. She's come a long way. Sometimes you just can't control where your brain takes your dreams." He knew that firsthand. He'd relived his childhood trauma of being locked in that fiery basement way too many times to count. And no matter how many times he revisited that terrible night, he always felt as if he was forgetting something. That unrecalled memory bothered him more than it should, and he had no idea why. Whatever it was must be worth blocking out. Too bad he couldn't forget the entire ordeal.

All the more reason to keep a close watch on Ava—if he hadn't made friends with those troublemakers at school, he'd never have gotten in that position in the first place.

"No, you definitely can't control everything." Caley looked away then, the wind ruffling her loose hair, and he hooked his thumbs in his belt loops so he wouldn't tuck the golden strands behind her ear. "I'll do whatever I can for her. My mom left when I was little, and I don't really remember her. But I still can hopefully relate to Ava."

The sad truth was, she probably would.

And he couldn't.

The night pressed around him then, suffocating, making it hard to breathe. Their casual rooftop conversation had gotten way too heavy, brought back too many memories best left buried. He'd hired Caley to be a babysitter and a part-time cook and housekeeper—not psychologist for him or his daughter. He knew her intentions were good, but probing into their hearts and pasts would only stir up more pain.

He'd had enough of that to last a lifetime.

"Ava is fine. We both are." Saying it multiple times didn't make it true, but in the sense that Caley was worried, they were doing okay. Neither of them grieved daily anymore. They'd gone on with their lives, as they must.

Their father-daughter relationship, however, was a different story. But Caley couldn't fix that any more than she could rewrite the past.

Or the future.

Brady gestured over his shoulder in the general direction of the ranch house. "I better get back. Have a good night."

"You, too. See you tomorrow." Caley smiled her goodbye but didn't make a move to go inside. She remained standing, staring at the stars.

Leaving Brady to wish, as he ambled away, that he could see what she did.

Chapter Five

She'd run into blazing buildings when others had run out. She'd skydived, steer wrestled and baby-sat for the world's most mischievous and trouble-making twin boys. She'd bungee jumped, rock climbed, white-water rafted and even won a jala-peño-eating contest in west Texas.

Walking inside a room at the local nursing home shouldn't be that difficult.

Caley stood just outside the doorway, breathing in the unmistakable smell of antiseptic mixed with a liberal spray of floral air freshener. She fought the urge to gag, to turn and run and pretend this wasn't happening. Nonie—*her* Nonie, trapped in a cream-colored prison. It wasn't fair.

But neither were a lot of things, including the way Caley had practically run away from home. And the way her dad and Nonie never seemed to care if she ever returned.

Hadn't anyone in her life ever truly wanted her? Her mom left them when Caley was young, choosing an older, wealthier man over her high-school-sweetheart husband, and never looked back.

Was Caley that forgettable?

"Is this the right room?" Ava tugged at Caley's shirtsleeve.

Caley startled, having nearly forgotten the girl was there. Not a great mark for her babysitting résumé. She shook her head to clear it and smiled down at her charge, hoping the younger girl didn't see how her lips shook of their own choosing. "Sorry. I zoned out there. This is right." But so, so wrong. She took a deep breath and urged her feet to move, but the brown cowboy boots refused to budge. "After you."

Ava furrowed her brow in confusion, but stepped around the door frame and into the room, leaving Caley no choice now but to follow.

The dim room, lit by the glare of a television playing an old game-show rerun, seemed depressing and suffocating. Nonie lay propped in bed, a half-empty glass of water next to her at the rolling bedside table, her eyes closed, mouth slightly open as she napped. The room had no pictures or flowers like some they'd passed in the hallway on their way here. No signs of life or love or cherished memories.

A knot formed in Caley's throat and threatened

to choke her completely. She coughed in an attempt to clear it, then covered her mouth with her hand, hoping she hadn't woken her grandmother. She couldn't do this right now. Not today. Maybe tomorrow.

Maybe the next day.

Memories blinded her, rushing at her in a wave of nostalgia thick enough to bottle. Nonie, surrounded by fabric squares as she pieced together a quilt. Nonie, handing Caley a freshly baked chocolate chip cookie and winking as she pressed a second one into her other hand. Nonie, rubbing her back when she was tired and holding her hair when she was sick.

Now Nonie was sick, and Caley couldn't do a thing about it.

She turned to escape, but her boot squeaked on the linoleum floor. Nonie's eyes fluttered open, and she stared at Caley as if she'd imagined her presence. Had she? Had she lain in this bed, feeble and frail and alone, imagining Caley there?

"Caley? Is that you?" The words bled from Nonie's throat, croaky and aged in a voice that wasn't her own.

Then she coughed, and her vibrancy returned as the frog vanished. "Girl, get over here. What took you so long? I've been waiting for weeks for you to show up."

Ava stared at Nonie and then at Caley, apparently searching for answers. Caley opened her mouth, then shut it and shrugged as she made her way to Nonie's bedside. "It's me."

Her grandmother's bony fingers cupped her shoulders in a hug, the pressure strong and tight like she'd always remembered. Caley pulled back, but Nonie held her close in a grip a pro wrestler would have admired. "You look good, kiddo."

"So do you." The words slipped out automatically before Caley could realize their lack of truth, but Nonie just laughed hard enough to bring on a coughing spell.

"Still full of jokes. Glad life hasn't beaten you down, my girl." Nonie clutched Caley's hand in her own veined, papery-thin one, and smiled, revealing perfect dentures. Then she leaned in closer, her wise blue gaze staring with the force of a laser. "Or has it?"

Caley tugged free, unable or maybe unwilling to answer. She wrapped one arm around Ava, who had dropped back, and propelled her forward. "Nonie, this is Ava. I'm her nanny for a few weeks. She and her dad live next door to the house I'm renting."

"I know this young'in from the church." Nonie latched on to Ava, who didn't seem to mind in the least. "McCollough, right?"

Ava nodded and returned the squeeze, even pumping Nonie's hand like she would a healthy adult with a regular handshake. "Nice to see you again, ma'am."

"I once changed your diapers in the church nursery." Nonie grinned, a flash of her former spunk still vivid in her eyes. She might be stuck in this bed, but her mind was certainly not the traitor her body was. "You and your daddy still attending?"

"Most weeks." Ava shrugged as she eased onto the side of the bed near Nonie. "We didn't for a long time, but I'm glad he takes me again. My Sunday-school class is fun."

"I sure wish they'd let me out of here to go." Nonie gestured to the room holding her captive. "But you know what's neat?" She leaned in close to Ava as if she had a secret, just like she'd done to Caley as a child. "I can meet with God right here in this room. Doesn't have to be in a church." She patted the worn Bible on the bedside table.

A muscle jumped in Caley's jaw. Nonie used to take her to church when she was growing up. Her father had refused to set foot in the building, for reasons she never fully understood.

Now she sort of got it.

Caley slipped away from the bed, gratefully allowing Nonie's attention to focus on Ava as they chattered about the people they knew in common from the church. It was a small world. No, small *town*. That was half the reason why Caley had bailed in the first place. She'd needed more space than four corners of a county line. More adventure than cow-tipping Farmer Ganshert's lazy herd on a Friday night.

More life than her dad would allow her to live.

"Been a long time." Nonie turned her attention Caley, her plum-colored lips thinning into a line. Leave it to Nonie to wear lipstick in the nursing home. Her eyes widened with meaning. "Too long."

"I'm sorry, Nonie." Caley started to say more, but the words froze deep inside and refused to thaw. Sudden tears burned behind her eyes, and she pinched the bridge of her nose to ward them off. It was her fault she'd stayed away—but then again, not entirely. "We should probably go." Far, far away. Where no one could see her cry or know her secrets. Know how selfish she'd been fresh out of high school. Know how she'd carried the hurt with her all over the country, nestled permanently on her back and heavier than the oxygen tank from her bunker gear.

But the scary part was—would she do it any differently if she could have a do-over?

"We just got here." Ava, with all the naivety and practicality of a preteen, perched on the edge of Nonie's bed. "*Wheel of Fortune* is coming on."

"I've gotten good at the puzzles." Nonie patted Ava's hand, and the cozy scene could have been a time warp from when Caley was ten years old, snuggled on Nonie's bed with the remote control and her favorite quilt. "But some puzzles, my dear, are not as easily solved."

Ava nodded as she tuned in to the show, but Caley knew those words were meant for her. She caught Nonie's eye over the top of Ava's head, and relaxed slightly at her grandmother's understanding wink. She sank into the hard wooden chair near the bed and leaned back, ignoring the way the slats dug into her back.

She deserved the pain.

Figured the one time Max went into town for feed, the bull got out.

Brady faced the hindquarters of the ornery steed from several yards away atop Nugget, who snorted and tossed his head, jangling the reins as if to say Brady must be crazy if he thought they were getting any closer to the loose animal. On his morning rounds, he'd noted the trampled section of barbed wire too late. Now his prized bull, Spitfire, was in open pasture, way too close to Caley's house—and the street—for comfort.

Brady fingered the lasso on his saddle horn, wondering if he should amble casually that direction or let the bull make the first move. Or, ideally, leave him be until Max returned as backup on a second horse. The bull wasn't outright dangerous in theory, but when trying to be coerced from greener pastures back into his section of pen, well…that could change. Already he shot wary, flat-eared glances at Nugget, as if he knew the horse's plans to round him up. At least Caley had taken Ava to the nursing home, so they weren't in the—

Gravel spun as Caley's truck pulled into her driveway. Brady winced as the commotion drew the bull's attention. His large black head popped up, grass dangling from his rubbery lips, and his tail stilled.

Caley and Ava climbed out, oblivious to the situation, their feminine voices carrying in the wind. Of all the times for them to go to Caley's house instead of the ranch. Scooter barked twice from inside the house, and Brady breathed his relief when Spitfire snorted in warning, then slowly returned to his afternoon snack. Good thing Caley had locked her dog up when they left earlier, or there'd be a three-ring circus in his pasture about now.

He turned in the saddle, the leather creaking beneath his weight, and waved one arm wildly to grab the girls' attention. They didn't see him. Then Ava slammed the car door, and Spitfire began to paw the ground.

Oh, no.

Sudden noises and anxious bulls went together, like—well, like a bull and fine china, or however that phrase went. Brady held his breath. Nugget, apparently sensing the same change in atmosphere as Brady, rolled the bit in his mouth and neighed deep in his throat. That was enough for Spitfire to charge.

Brady jerked the reins to turn Nugget around and nudged him with his heels, but fortunately the horse needed little encouragement to bolt. Unfortunately, he headed straight for the fence separating his property from Caley's rental.

Unpleasant options flashed through his mind. He could bail and probably injure himself in a roll—or he could hang on. The fence drew nearer, as did the pounding of hooves behind them. Making the only decision that he could, Brady dropped the reins to give Nugget his head, grabbed the saddle horn and welded his legs to Nugget's sides as they went airborne.

They landed with a thud that jarred Brady's teeth, and in his peripheral vision he glimpsed Spitfire careening to a stop just short of the fence. He grabbed the dangling reins and urged the horse to stop on the other side of Caley's driveway and turn around, grateful the chase was over.

Spitfire butted the fence with his head twice before snorting his disdain, then snagged a handful of weeds from under the bottom slat with his teeth and ambled off. He'd gotten the last word, and he knew it. Rounding him up would be ten times harder now.

"That was awesome." Ava's voice suddenly sounded from Brady's knee, and he looked down to see her wide eyes shining with admiration. She rubbed Nugget's sweaty neck, and Brady caught his breath long enough to reach down and do the same.

"Thanks, I think." *Awesome* might not be the word he'd been envisioning, but his relief clogged his frustration for now. Mostly. He started to order Ava inside the house, wanting a locked door and a lot of brick between her and Spitfire, when Caley joined them.

"Nice jump." She shaded her eyes with her head as she peered up at him, her free hand reaching out to scratch Nugget under the chin. The horse dipped his head to rest in her grip, and Brady suddenly wished he had the right to snuggle up to her, too. "For a cowboy, anyway." She winked. "Now you know why professional jumpers use English saddles."

No, now he just thought professional jumpers were crazy to jump without a saddle horn. He swung down, his legs suffering from the wild burst of adrenaline, and stomped his feet a few times to get the feeling back. "I want you both to go in the house and stay there. I've got to try to get that beast back to his pasture before he decides the grass looks even greener across the street."

"By yourself?" Caley's brow crinkled. "Is that a good idea?"

Brady wiped sweat from his forehead with his shirtsleeve. "Can't wait for Max to get back now. Spitfire's too close to the road. That fence won't hold him if he gets angry again, and if he wanders too far on the other side of that meadow, he'll get out that way."

"Let me help. I know how to ride." Caley tossed her purse on the hood of her car as if ready to saddle up that minute. "Ava can wait for me inside. I can drive back to the ranch and grab another horse—"

"No." He bit the word off sharper than he meant to, but Caley had to be several cows short of a herd if she thought he'd let her anywhere near that ornery beast. "I'll do it."

She crossed her arms over her chest. "Don't be ridiculous. I'll stay in the back, and just be a deterrent for him not to run off to the side while you direct him. That's what Max would do, right?"

Yes, but Max was a hired hand, and made of tough stock—and more importantly, not Brady's responsibility. He crossed his own arms, mirroring her defensive stance. "A deterrent—and a distraction. Spitfire could just as easily charge you as he did me."

"Then it's a good thing you demonstrated such fabulous jumping skills." A spark lit her eyes, one that held sass and even a little bit of longing. Caley *wanted* to risk her life to round up a stray bull? That didn't match up with what he knew of her so far.

Though it did sort of match up with the lady he'd met last night on the roof.

Brady swung back into the saddle. Now wasn't the time to figure out the puzzle that made up his new neighbor. Now was the time to get his four-legged major source of income back into the right pen.

Alone.

He adjusted his hat, then picked up the reins. "Sorry. But no."

The disappointment in both Caley's and Ava's eyes twisted his gut, but he held his mouth steady and nudged Nugget with his boots. They'd have to go the long way around, since he didn't particularly want to urge his mount over that fence a second time. Nor could he risk startling Spitfire again.

He glanced back at Caley and Ava, still planted in the driveway near the truck. "In the house, ladies." He gestured over his shoulder toward her rental, wishing he'd passed down to Ava something besides his own stubborn streak. He swallowed hard. "Please."

That did the trick. Caley picked up her purse and ushered Ava inside the house. He waited until the door shut firmly behind them before he turned back in the saddle and directed Nugget around the perimeter of the fence. There was a gate about a hundred yards around the bend. He'd slip in that way and come up behind the bull, then hopefully drive him back toward his separate pen. Of course, it'd help if he had a horse that wasn't afraid of the beast.

Brady cast a glance back at Caley's rental, and sighed.

And it'd help even more if he had a nanny who was.

Chapter Six

Apparently there was something in Broken Bend's water that made smart people oblivious to truth.

Caley slung her purse on the counter, fighting the urge to look out the window that glimpsed Brady's back pasture and make sure he was all right. If he wanted to try to do something foolish, like round up a bull—that'd already spooked his horse once—by himself, then so be it. The risk of someone getting hurt was greater with him out there alone than with someone's help, even hers. But the men of Broken Bend apparently drank a little more of that bayou stubbornness than others.

Her dad had certainly gulped his share.

"Is he going to be okay?" Ava's drawn voice sounded from the living room, where she'd peeled back the thin curtains and stared into the field. Scooter pressed against her side in sympathy,

whining. He'd always been able to tell when someone was worried.

Caley's frustration at being held back faded at
the worry in Ava's tone. "Of course, sweetie. Your
dad knows what he's doing." She believed that, but
it still stung that he didn't think enough of her to
believe her own ability. But why did it matter so
much?

She swallowed against the answer beating in
her heart.

Because she wanted the man on the roof—the
one who'd sat with her despite his obvious dislike
of heights, the one who'd ask her about her grandmother and didn't push when she'd verbally shut
down, the one who'd shared the moonlight—to
like her.

Respect her.

And not just as a nanny.

Caley ran the edges of the curtain through her
fingers, the flimsy fabric cool against her palm.
Maybe she'd taken in some of that bayou water
herself. Because no matter how attractive Brady
was or how good-hearted he appeared to be, she
wasn't the Broken Bend woman he needed. Even
if she could fix the cracks in his family, he made
it clear last night that he didn't want her to. *Ava is
fine. We both are.*

She could tell that wasn't true.

But she'd pretty much written the book on

denial, so how much of a hypocrite would she be if she pressed him about it?

"There he goes." Ava's voice broke through Caley's thoughts, freeing her from the relentless possibilities of what could be and what wouldn't ever be. "Dad's trying to go in behind him."

Caley edged closer to Ava as she peered through the glass over her head, Scooter's tail thumping a steady rhythm against her leg. Was that a lasso? Was Brady really going to try to rope the bull? Seemed crazy, but on second thought, she'd heard from firemen who took side jobs as rodeo clowns that oftentimes when an animal got a wild hair, all they needed was a firm hand and direction to bring them back around. Maybe that was Brady's plan.

Not a bad one, but it'd be a whole lot better if he'd wait for Max.

She exhaled with relief, not even realizing until that moment she'd been holding her breath. "Spitfire doesn't see him yet."

"Nope. Is that good or bad?" Ava glanced up at her.

"Could be either." She licked her suddenly dry lips as Spitfire's head rose from the grass just as Brady began to wind his rope. Then, without warning, the bull whipped around and pawed the earth. "Never mind. Not good."

It was too much for Nugget. The horse reared,

and even from this distance, Caley could tell Brady wasn't ready. His arms windmilled with the lasso as he fought for balance, but his horse was too fast. He barreled off the back of Nugget and landed hard on the packed ground as the horse bolted away.

Ava shrieked, clasping both hands to her mouth, and Caley's heart leaped in her throat with the force of a jackhammer. "Wait here."

She burst through the front door, slamming it behind her to show Ava she meant business about staying put, and ran as fast as she could toward the fence separating her from Brady. She prayed for the first time in too long, the words whipping through her head as fast as the grass whipping past her boots. *God, Ava needs her daddy. Don't take him, too.* She didn't think she was in a position to ask for any favors, but if there was ever any grace to be found, surely it would land on a sweetheart like Ava.

Thankfully, Spitfire had taken off after Nugget again, leaving Brady time to gather himself. But he wasn't leaping immediately to his feet. She hoped he hadn't hit his head.

"Brady!" She cupped her hands and hollered as loud as she could. He staggered to his knees, blood dripping from a cut on his brow, answering her question. She caught her breath, hope filling her heart at the sight of him moving, albeit slowly.

"Are you okay?" Her legs trembled beneath her, willing his reply.

He lifted one hand as if to tell her to wait, his other fist pounding his chest. He'd probably gotten the wind knocked out of him, and Caley knew from ladder-training mishaps that took a minute to recover from. Not to mention it hurt like crazy.

Across the field, Spitfire—apparently tired of chasing Nugget, who appeared to be heading back toward the barn—focused his attention toward Brady, still at half-mast in the field. He saw the danger the same time she did, and he began hurrying toward the fence.

But he wasn't fast enough.

Caley might not be able to control the future, but she sure wasn't going to stand by and let Ava become an orphan today. Without hesitation, she hauled herself over the fence and slipped two fingers in her mouth, whistling loud enough to perk the ears of every horse in the neighboring counties.

Just as she'd hoped, Spitfire changed direction and barreled toward her, wide nostrils flaring to twice their size. Brady darted toward the fence, ninety degrees from Spitfire, steering clear of the bull's peripheral vision. Caley hooked one foot on the fence and swung her leg over toward safety, heart pounding in her ears. Spitfire hadn't jumped it the first time. Hopefully he wouldn't be further motivated now.

She cleared the fence, noting Brady had done the same, and landed hard, dropping to one knee in the grass. Brady, still running, pointed to her truck. "Bed." The word rasped out barely louder than her heartbeat in her ears.

Sudden hooves pounded behind her, and Caley decided she didn't want to trust Spitfire's previous decisions after all. She propped one foot on the fender of her pickup and Brady grabbed her arms, hauling her over the tailgate. He pulled her down into the bed of the truck just as Spitfire crashed through the fence, sending a shower of wood splinters raining around them.

Caley covered her head, and Brady's breath fanned her cheek, his arms wrapped with firm pressure around her shoulders. "Stay down."

Angry snorts sounded from near the wheel well, and Caley willingly obeyed, moving only the elbow that she knew dug into Brady's ribs.

"When they lose visual, they calm down." His voice whispered in her ear, husky and warm, and his heart pounded a matching rhythm against her palm, still resting on his chest.

Caley quickly moved her hand, face flaming. She wasn't entirely sure which was more terrifying—the close call they'd just had, or the feelings being in such close proximity to Brady stirred in her heart. "Is it safe?" It felt anything but, for myriad reasons.

Brady gently shifted her off him and propped up on one elbow, just enough to peer over the rim of the bed. The blood on his forehead had dried to rust, smearing the corner of his temple. "He's back in the pasture now, seems calm." He pushed up on his knees and stood, then reached down to help propel Caley to her feet.

She brushed off the back of her jeans, and Brady plucked a piece of wood shaving from her hair. Their eyes locked and held, and Brady's finger grazed her cheek before he dropped his hand to his side. "That was dangerous."

No kidding. She still couldn't breathe, and it wasn't because of Spitfire. She tried to look away from his arresting gaze, but failed. "I know. You almost got yourself killed."

Brady broke eye contact then, folding his arms over his wrinkled and torn shirt. "I meant you. I told you and Ava to stay inside."

"Why, so we could watch through the window as you got yourself gored?" All traces of the chemistry that had previously pulsed between them vanished as indignation took its place. Caley reached up and tapped Brady's head, beside his cut. "Exhibit A."

"I would have been fine." His lips thinned and

frustration sparked in his blue eyes, so similar to Ava's. "Just got the breath knocked out of me."

"Which wouldn't have been a big deal—if there hadn't been a bull charging you at the same time." Caley pushed past Brady, checked to make sure Spitfire was a safe distance away and hiked her leg over the tailgate. She slid to the ground as frustration welled inside. She'd worked with some pretty macho guys over the course of her career, but this one took the cake. "Why are you being so stubborn?"

Brady landed on the ground beside her. "Me being stubborn?" He jabbed his chest, his eyebrows hiking up his forehead and wrinkling the fresh cut. The sudden motion had to hurt, but to his credit, he didn't even flinch. "You're the one being stubborn. Your job is to protect my daughter."

"And I did." Caley stalked toward the back door, pausing with her hand on the knob. She shot him a look over her shoulder. "I protected her from having to watch her father die."

He'd known Caley Foster was going to be trouble. Hadn't he declared it from day one?

Brady slapped the dust off his cowboy hat before planting it back on his head. The comforting aroma of hay and horse sweat filled the barn around him, accompanied by the familiar sounds of jangling harnesses and horse tails swishing at flies—but all he could hear was the echoing snort of Spitfire's wrath. The heaviness of his hooves.

The disdain in Caley's voice as she leveled her last barb directly at his heart.

He wasn't stubborn. He was *careful*. Caley didn't understand—he'd lost someone he loved because of his carelessness in the past. He wouldn't let that happen to his daughter, or anyone else in his charge, ever again.

Even if that cost him his own life.

But it hadn't. He'd had it under control. If anything, she'd scared ten years from him the way she ran out in the pasture, whistling like some kind of Annie Oakley fresh off the range. Who was this woman, anyway? What happened to the cookie-baking—well, cookie-*attempting*—grandmother-visiting, sweet-smiling role model he'd hired? This woman camped out on roofs, ran faster than he could, faced off with bulls and shinnied up and down ladders and fences like they weren't even there. Not exactly role-model material for a daughter he was trying to keep safe.

Unfortunately, that didn't stop the way he'd reacted to Caley's nearness in the truck, the way he'd appreciated the warmth of her against him, the way he'd pulled fence shavings from her hair and had to stop himself from curling those silky golden strands through his fingers and leaning in to kiss the worry from her brow.

Yep, Caley Foster was out-and-out trouble.

"Guess I shouldn't go pick up feed anymore." Max's voice teased from down the barn as he emerged from the tack room, thankfully distracting Brady from the details of his adventure he'd be smart to forget. "You'll just set the ranch on fire or something."

"Very funny. Keep your day job." Brady rolled his eyes at his friend, but his ire didn't run deep. Max had really helped him out. He'd driven up at the ranch just as Brady had hiked back to corral Nugget and go after Spitfire again. Max had joined him on another horse, and together, they'd put the bull back in his own pasture and quick-fixed his fence. The temporary repair would hold now that Spitfire wasn't on the rampage, but now Brady had two fences to mend.

Caley's angry, hurt expression flashed in his mind, and he sighed. Make that three.

Max braced his forearms on Nugget's low stall door next to Brady. "Well, the tack is rubbed down, boss." He paused and studied Brady. "You might want to go clean that gash on your head next."

"It's not that bad. Nugget just happened to dump me on a rock." Brady reached up to touch the tender flesh, a knot forming beneath the wound and sending a headache pulsing through his temples and down his neck. It did need some soap and water, but heading inside to clean it now seemed like defeat. Like admitting Caley was right.

Like the way it hurt to take a deep breath meant she really had saved his life.

"Jokes aside, I'm glad it worked out okay. I had no idea Nugget was so skittish with Spitfire. Could have been really bad." Max lifted his hand from the stall wall and winced. "Splinter."

"I didn't know, either. Wish I could have found out a little easier." He reached up to pat Nugget's cheek. "Speaking of splinters, we need to get Caley's fence fixed ASAP, since Spitfire mauled it. Don't want her landlord having a heart attack if he comes by to check on the property." He rubbed grit from his eyes and wished he could just go inside and take a few pain pills and a nap. But the work at the ranch wouldn't do itself. "You know how particular Tommy is."

"Doesn't the entire town." Max picked at his callused palm. "Man, I hate splinters."

So did Brady. Hated the kind that nestled unwillingly under his skin, the kind that poked and prodded tender areas best left ignored. The kind with blond hair and too much ambition for their own good.

The kind he was going to have to apologize to.

Chapter Seven

Three days. Caley had only worked as Ava's nanny for three days, and already she'd intermittently wanted to strangle and—if she was painfully honest—kiss the girl's father.

Neither was the smartest of options.

Across the dining room table, Ava hunched over her homework, mumbling definitions under her breath and occasionally scrawling something in a notebook. Caley folded another bath towel and added it to the growing stack, trying unsuccessfully to ignore the sight of Brady through the kitchen window, strolling in and out of the barn. She had no clue how one girl and one man could go through so much laundry, but somehow she'd folded two loads of towels alone in the three days she'd been there.

Too bad she couldn't roll one up and smack Brady with it.

He had yet to speak to her since the incident with Spitfire yesterday, staying out past dinnertime to repair the fence, and then passing through the house with his head down and offering only curt sentences to Ava before heading for the shower. She'd arrived at the house just in time for Ava to ride the bus home from school that afternoon, and had yet to see him up close. Either he was majorly busy undoing Spitfire's damage, or he was avoiding her.

And if it was the latter, it was only because he knew she'd been right, and he couldn't admit it.

"What's the definition for the word *aplomb?*" Ava scratched her head with her pencil, messing up her ponytail. "I've got to match them up and I don't have a clue."

"Let me think. English was never my best subject. I was more of a math girl growing up." Caley slipped behind Ava's chair and took out the hair band, smoothing the top of her hair flat before resecuring it. "*Aplomb.* I think it means bravery."

Ava read the choices on her sheet, then pointed to one in the far column. "This is it, then. Self-confidence or assurance?"

"Bingo." Caley slapped her a high five and then returned to the towels, this time sitting down and curling her bare feet up under her. "Good job."

"Too bad I don't have to use it in a sentence." Ava lowered her voice as if reading a headline.

"Young girl's nanny shows major aplomb when rounding up a wild bull."

Caley laughed as she straightened the teetering pile of washcloths. "That'd get you an A for sure." Too bad Brady wouldn't think so. Of all the words he'd use to describe Caley, she felt pretty certain that *aplomb* wouldn't be on the list.

Of course, she had a few choice words for him as well, so maybe that was fair.

But nothing was fair about him shutting her out, ignoring what they'd experienced yesterday. Right or wrong, they'd lived through an adventure, and she thought they'd connected in those charged moments in her truck. Was he going to pretend it hadn't happened? Well, she could do that, too. Denial was her specialty.

She just needed to know what the rules were, so her stomach could quit flipping in circles every time she glimpsed him outside the big bay windows.

"Is supper almost ready?" Ava set down her pencil and pressed her hand against her stomach. "My tummy's growling."

The timer dinged from the other side of kitchen in response.

"I'd say that's a yes." She shooed Ava off to go wash her hands in the bathroom, and hurried to peer inside the oven. The casserole she'd made for their supper looked done—maybe a little too done. She grabbed an oven mitt and pulled the large dish out to check its crispness just as Brady opened the back door.

He stomped his boots on the braided rug in the entryway, but Caley refused to look at him or acknowledge he'd come inside. Two could play whatever immature game he'd been playing, and she'd play to win. He'd made it clear he wanted her *serving* them, not actually participating in their lives. Fine with her. She set the casserole on the stove top—it would do, well-done or not—and shut the oven door, pulling off the mitt, and grabbed a serving spoon.

"Smells good."

His deep voice filled the kitchen and sent unwanted shivers down her spine. She ignored him and the way his boots thudded toward her as he crossed the room and began to wash his hands in the kitchen sink. She dipped the spoon into the chicken and rice, turned the burner off under the pot of green beans and started pulling plates from the cabinet by the sink, uncannily aware of every move he made.

The water shut off. "Let me help."

Oh, *now* he was Mr. Nice Guy. His damp hands interrupted hers reaching for the forks in the silverware drawer, and she jerked back, refusing to answer. She grabbed the knives instead and stacked them on the plates, then tore several paper towels from the roll on the counter and carried the lot of it to the table.

"Caley?"

She whirled around, not expecting him to be directly behind her, and bumped into his hard chest, a solid mound of muscle. Their cozy, unexpected moment together in the truck flashed through her mind and she quickly started to back away, unwilling to tease herself with the memory another second. But he grabbed her arms and held her in place. "Will you be still? I need to tell you something."

Oh, she was sure he had plenty more lectures up his sleeve about danger and safety and obeying the rules to the detriment of others. But she wasn't paid to listen to them.

She tugged free, and he let her go, despite the pleading in his eyes. "I don't think you do." She began clearing Ava's homework from the table, wishing she could just toss the casserole on the table and bail. But she wouldn't leave without giving Ava a hug goodbye, and the girl still hadn't returned from the bathroom. She met Brady's eyes briefly as she crossed the kitchen to get the casserole. "You've said plenty already, trust me." And in other ways, not nearly enough.

She grabbed the hot pan just as she realized she hadn't put the oven mitt back on. Heat scorched her fingers, and she dropped the dish by reflex.

The glass shattered to the floor, sending a tidal wave of overcooked chicken and rice across the tiles—and around her bare feet.

"Don't move!" Brady jumped to her side, glass crunching under his boots, and scooped her up in his arms. The aroma of horse and hay and lemon soap wafted through her shock, drawing her in. She clutched the front of his work shirt in her uninjured hand, not caring about the dust and tiny white horsehairs that covered the material, and held on tight as he carried her to the kitchen table.

He deposited her on top of it, not appearing to care as a tower of her carefully folded towels toppled off and landed on the floor. He rushed to the freezer and returned with a bag of frozen peas. If she looked at the undoing of her hard work on the floor—either in fabric form or rice form—she'd cry. So she just looked helplessly into his eyes. They appeared compassionate. Concerned.

Big mistake.

Tears formed anyway, and she clutched the bag of peas to her chest, the cold seeping through her shirt and distracting her from the pain in her fingers. She wished Brady would just go back to ignoring her. Arguing and having a stubborn match was a whole lot easier to deal with than this nice guy before her. This hero.

Who apparently didn't think enough of her to trust her opinions or advice. And why should he?

She couldn't even bake cookies or get supper on the table without catastrophe.

Pity parties weren't normally her style, but this one was settling in and getting comfortable.

She fought the urge to break down completely, closing her eyes as Brady wiped a lingering tear from her cheek. "Does it hurt that bad?"

Yes, but in more ways than he realized. Still, at least he thought her pain was from the burn and not the totally uncharacteristic flurry of emotions fluttering through her heart. When was the last time she'd even been on a date? Had it been so long that her heart was desperately reaching out for company? Any company?

No. It was Brady. She'd been drawn to him from the moment he first crossed their dividing property line and shook her hand with his work-worn one.

The one that still lingered by her cheek.

She leaned away from his touch and removed the bag of peas to study her red fingers. "I'll be all right. It's just a first-degree burn."

Brady gingerly took her hand, as if to determine her diagnosis himself. "I think you're right."

Of course she was. She was a firefighter and a certified EMT. Why couldn't she be attracted to a man who had more in common with her? One who wasn't grounded to this particular piece of earth like a thirty-year-old oak? One who didn't raise his own child the way her father had raised her? Stifled. Cared for, but ignored in the ways that mattered most to a girl.

One who actually took her opinions and advice seriously and treated her as an equal.

On closer inspection, she really had no reason to feel the way she did about Brady and all of the above reasons *not* to.

But try telling that to the can-can dancers kicking across her stomach.

"I was trying to tell you a minute ago that I was sorry. You were right about Spitfire, and I was being stubborn. I just didn't want you or Ava to get hurt." Brady tucked the bag of peas back over her burn, glancing up to make eye contact.

Sorry. He was apologizing? Maybe there were more reasons to feel for Brady than she'd thought. When was the last time a man had ever apologized to her? In her field, it didn't happen often. The firemen she'd worked with over the years were mostly good men, but certainly gave new definition to the term *macho*. The most she'd ever gotten was a grunt of acknowledgment for being right.

But Brady was saying the words. And, from the look in his eyes, meaning them.

"But then you decided to throw my supper on the floor, so I guess we're even." He winked, and her heart dipped into her toes.

"Thank you." She licked her dry lips, wishing

she had the words to express how much his apology really meant to her. But opening her heart to that degree wouldn't be helpful for either of them. Best to keep it light. "And, well, I'm sorry about your dinner."

Together they stared at the heap of overly crisped food and glass on the floor, and Brady began to laugh. "Would it make things better or worse if I told you I'm a little relieved?"

Caley removed the peas long enough to smack his bicep with the dripping, defrosting bag. "Worse." She grinned, then shrieked as he swiped the bottom of the bag and wiped the condensation across her cheek. "Cut it out!" Laughing, she reached for revenge, then stopped at the sight of Ava in the doorway.

"What in the world?" Ava braced against the frame, her eyes roving across the casserole, the glass and the pile of towels. They darted between Brady and Caley twice before coming to rest on the melting bag of peas.

Brady took a quick step back from the table, and Caley took her first deep breath since being in his proximity. She offered Ava a sheepish smile. "There was a little mishap with the casserole."

Ava narrowed her eyes with suspicion—and hope. "Does this mean we're ordering a pizza?"

"Why not?" Brady took the bag of peas from

Caley and tossed it in the sink. "Grab the phone. I'll get a large with everything."

Ava scrambled for the phone as Brady grabbed a broom from the pantry and began to sweep the glass.

This was all her fault, and yet she was sitting helpless on the table. Some nanny she was. "Let me get my shoes on and I'll help." Caley hopped down from the table, wincing as her thawing finger began to throb with the sudden motion.

"Oh, no. I think you've done enough." Brady tossed her a rogue grin over his shoulder as he swept.

And Caley realized she was in very real danger of getting burned a second time.

Brady opened the refrigerator door, light puddling on the ground at his bare feet and illuminating a shard of glass he'd missed during cleanup earlier that evening. He plucked it from the floor and tossed it in the trash can, then returned to the box of leftover pizza.

Caley hadn't stayed for supper, claiming she needed to get home and tend to her fingers. He'd offered to help her do first aid with the burn cream in his bathroom cabinet, but she'd tossed him a funny look and assured him she had everything she needed at home. He knew she'd said before that she was a certified EMT, but that didn't necessarily mean she kept a bunch of supplies at her house. Oh, well. Of all the things puzzling about Caley, that was the probably the least so.

He picked the remaining slice from the box and bit into it cold, wishing she had stayed for supper. Mary hadn't ever stayed, but this situation was obviously different.

And that's why Brady was standing in front of the open fridge at midnight, once again unable to sleep. If he didn't figure out how he felt about Caley soon, he'd be useless on the ranch. He definitely couldn't afford to let that happen, yet every time he tried to sleep, her face filled his eyes, her laughter teasing the silence in the recesses of his mind. He knew better than to go for a stroll tonight to clear his head, in case he ran into her again on her roof. Another close encounter under the stars and he'd be toast.

Would it be terrible if he asked her out?

The question had taunted him for days, escalating to a pitch he couldn't ignore after rescuing her this afternoon. Normally he'd forbid himself, since she was an employee of his, but as Max had uncouthly pointed out, that was only temporary.

But Caley seemed to have a feisty side that didn't match with his lifestyle—and more importantly, the lifestyle he was trying so hard to create for Ava.

Brady shut the fridge and finished his pizza

in the dark, staring out the kitchen window at his moonlit fields. Was he truly ready to date? He hadn't done more than a casual dinner with a woman since Jessica's death, and even that had been hard. During the entire meal, his thoughts had been consumed with Ava and the past and what he was missing at the ranch, rather than staying focused on his companion.

But somehow he couldn't imagine himself being so distracted if he was sitting across from Caley.

Well, he had to do something. No doubt the spark he felt went both ways. He'd recognized it in her touch, seen it in her eyes as they'd huddled in the truck and as he carried her across the kitchen in his arms. She'd say yes.

Hopefully.

He tossed the end of the burned pizza crust into the trash can and wiped his hands on his pajama pants. The worst that could happen was she'd say no, and he'd deal with that if it came up. It'd make things awkward, but he'd already proven he could stay away from her outside if need be. Of course, they'd probably have to wait until Mary got back to go out, because who could he get to stay with Ava?

Brady headed toward his room, his thoughts racing as if he'd run a marathon instead of shuffled across the rug to his bed. Maybe he should wait until Mary got back, anyway—if he did, he'd solve the babysitter problem and the no-dating-your-employee problem at the same time. Plus, that'd give him a few more weeks to get to know Caley and make sure he wasn't leaping before he looked, or however that went.

He slid between his cool sheets and stretched out, finally finding a measure of peace at having a plan. He'd leap, all right. Caley seemed more than worth it.

He'd just look real hard first.

Chapter Eight

❧

"How's the mare?" Brady stopped outside Lady's stall, where Max was brushing down the expecting mare, and reached over the short door to rub her sandy neck.

Max dropped the brush in the grooming bucket at his feet and clapped his hands on his jeans. Dust formed a cloud around his legs. He grinned. "Dirty."

"She's been scratching her back again." Brady opened the stall door and ran a hand over the mare's swollen belly. She nickered, and her belly shifted with the weight of the foal inside. "Won't be long now. I'll let the vet know."

"Better you than me." Max grabbed the bucket and exited the stall. "I don't think she's forgiven me yet."

Brady's hand stilled on the mare, and frustration welled in his throat. Hopefully his friend was kidding. "Dr. Peters?"

"In my defense, when we went out years ago, she was still just Rachel Peters." Max shifted the bucket to his other hand. "She apparently expected a call back from me after our last date, and, well…" His voice trailed off.

"Max. Our vet? Really?" Brady shut the stall door and clanked the latch down with more force than necessary. "Why didn't you tell me?"

Max shrugged. "I didn't think she cared. It was years ago. But I saw her in town the other day, and it was awkward—at best."

"So that's why you always leave the ranch when she comes by to check the animals." Brady ran one hand over his brow, adjusting his hat and wishing he could take it off and smack his friend with it. "Seriously, you can't alienate the entire female population in town. You already have a reputation."

Max walked backward toward the tack room, grinning. "Hey, if you don't connect with someone, you don't connect. Not my fault I just keep trying." He turned and set the grooming bucket inside the tack room. "And speaking of connecting, don't pretend like you've not got something for the nanny. I saw you carrying her through the kitchen last night. You know your windows are made of glass, right?"

A slow burn started in Brady's chest, partially from the irritation of his friend's nosiness, and partially from the memory of holding Caley close. "She burned herself cooking dinner, is all. I had to carry her away from the broken glass."

Max shut the tack room door. "Didn't you say she burned the cookies she made, too?"

Now it was Brady's turn to shrug. Forget a water break. He should have just stayed outside with Nugget and gone on to check the fences in the south forty. "Who cares? She's doing her job. Ava doesn't need too many sweets, anyway."

"But maybe you do." Max knuckled him on the shoulder. "Right, boss?"

He knew his friend meant well and was just teasing, but it rankled. Probably because Max was right. "Look, I'm not going to lie. I'm attracted to her."

Max let out a whoop, startling several horses and creating a series of restless whinnies up and down the aisle. "It's about time! So, when you going to ask her out?"

"It's not that easy for me, okay? I have a lot to think about here." He headed toward the barn door, leaving Max no choice but to hush or follow. Unfortunately, he followed.

"Like what? How pretty she is?"

Brady strode outside into the afternoon sunlight, where he'd left Nugget's reins looped around the fence post. "Like, I have a daughter. And I'm a widower."

That shut Max up. He hesitated before responding. "Look, you know I just want to see you happy, right? It's been a long time, man."

"I know." Brady untied Nugget's rope with short, jerky movements. "And Caley's great. She seems to be what Ava needs—stable, a good influence."

Max quirked an eyebrow. "What about what you need?"

He let out a long breath as he glanced up toward the house. "That, too." He hoped. In every way, Caley seemed the ideal match for both him and Ava. Sweet. Hard working. Safe. Well, there *was* the situation with the bull, but looking back, he could see Caley's desire to protect. Besides, what were the odds a situation like that would come up again?

Still…

Brady looped Nugget's rope over the fence and climbed up in the saddle. "For Ava's sake, I just have to be sure." More like absolutely certain— and maybe for his own sake, too. Taking risks wasn't his thing. Max knew that, but for some reason, he kept pushing.

He latched on to the excuse he'd given Max back on Caley's first day instead. "It's awkward, with Caley being my employee. There's a lot of factors going on here, and I don't know what she's thinking." To put it mildly. Had anyone *ever* known what went on beneath those sparkling eyes and teasing smile?

He just knew he wanted to find out.

Max leaned against the fence railing, hooking his thumbs in his front pockets as he grinned up at him. "Want me to talk to her for you?"

Brady snorted. "What is this, junior high? Just grab me some water, okay? I need to go check that fence. After Spitfire's incident, I'm not taking any more chances." At all. Especially not with Caley. He'd move on his own time.

But he couldn't help smiling at the realization that it seemed as though that time was getting pretty close.

"Do you think Nonie will like this?" Ava held up the drawing she'd made with colored pencils, hope lighting her expression.

Caley turned off the water at the kitchen sink, having finished hand washing the larger pots that wouldn't fit in the dishwasher, and gave Ava's picture a thorough study. The sketch contained grassy hills shaded with forest-green and dotted with purple wildflowers, along with a bright yellow sun with orange swirls and a square red barn standing ground in the corner. A black dog that could only be Scooter stood guard near the barn door.

"That's really impressive. I think Nonie will love it." She dried her hands, then carefully picked up the drawing. "Is this the view outside?" She glanced out the kitchen windows and Ava nodded.

"I wanted to do the clouds, too, but the paper is already white." She took the drawing back from Caley and smoothed it on the table in front of her.

"Why don't you color the sky blue, and just leave patches of white paper as the clouds?"

Ava frowned as the words sank in, then her face lit as recognition dawned. "That's perfect! Thanks, Miss Caley!" She grabbed the corn-flower-blue pencil and began to shade in the sky.

Too bad all of life's problems weren't as easily solved. Nonie would love the drawing when they went to visit her the next day, would probably even hang it on the bulletin board by her bed, remind-ing Caley of all the pictures she'd drawn for her growing up. Every time one made the refrigera-tor, it was as if she'd won a prize.

Caley picked up the pink pencil and ran her fingers over the trim wood. A part of her itched to return to childhood, before things got so com-plicated with her father and with life in general, and draw amateur sketches for her grandmother.

The other part of her still feared she'd never make the fridge again.

She set the pencil down just as the back door opened. Max, Brady's ranch hand, ambled in-side, pausing to wipe his boots on the rug. His hair, lighter brown than Brady's, was mostly covered by a cowboy hat. He stomped twice and his spurs jingled.

"Uncle Max!" Ava leaped from her seat, wrapped her arms around Max's middle, squeezing tight, and buried her face in his striped work shirt.

"Hey, kiddo." Max ruffled Ava's hair. "What are y'all up to in here?"

"Drawing." Ava darted to the table and proudly held up her sketch. "What do you think? It's for Caley's grandmother in the nursing home."

Max shot Caley a wink, then turned an approving smile at Ava. "I think she'll have the best-decorated room in the entire joint."

Ava grinned, cheeks flushed happily, and went back to finishing the sky and clouds.

Max held out his hand to Caley. "I'm Max Ringgold. I don't think Brady let me officially introduce myself yet."

What did he mean, let him? "Caley Foster." She shook his hand, his grip similar to Brady's and lined with calluses. But while Max oozed charm from every dirt-covered pore, he didn't have Brady's sincere eyes—or his smile, for that matter. She narrowed her eyes in suspicion, but Max didn't seem to notice as he strode to the refrigerator.

"We needed some water. The dorm fridge in the barn is empty." Max snagged several bottles from inside and shut the door with his heel. "And I thought any excuse to meet *the* Caley Foster was a great one."

Caley fought the urge to roll her eyes. He'd won points with her when he'd exclaimed over Ava's hard work. It was obvious the girl drank in praise like rain seeped into the desert sands. But he was losing those points quick. "I'm not that spectacular, don't worry."

Max leaned against the fridge, appearing to be in no hurry to get back to the barn with the water. "That's not what I hear."

Had Brady been discussing her with Max? And if so, in what way? Surely just in regard to Ava and the way she'd connected with the girl during her week of babysitting. Surely not anything more.

She decided to keep it light, just in case. Crossing her arms, she mimicked his overly casual pose. "Then did you hear about the inedible cookies and the burned casserole?" Definitely not spectacular. In fact, she was a little surprised after the incident with Spitfire and lack of ability in the kitchen that Brady hadn't let her go. He must be more desperate with Mary gone than she'd realized.

Max snorted back a laugh, his eyes lighting. But they still didn't do to her stomach what Brady's intense gaze did. "I did, actually. But don't worry. Ava isn't the only one who thinks you're awesome."

She definitely didn't miss *that* insinuation.

Max continued before she could figure out how to respond. "So what's next for you? After this gig is up, I mean." He gestured with a bottle to Ava, who had finished her picture and started a new one with the red-colored pencil.

"I'm hoping to get hired at district one." She sat down across from Ava, putting even more distance between her and Max. She knew he was harmless, but the last thing she wanted was for him to think she was flirting back.

"The fire station?" Genuine surprise filled Max's voice, followed by a slow grin that slid up his cheeks. "You're a firefighter?"

"Yep!" Ava piped up as she scribbled on her new drawing. "She's got a T-shirt and a real pager and everything."

She held a hand over her mouth to hide her smile at the pride highlighting Ava's voice. It was as if the younger girl had taken ownership in Caley's interests. Fine by her—maybe she'd be a better example to Ava than she'd originally hoped. If the only female role model in Ava's life was an elderly lady, Caley would gladly display the role of a strong, independent young woman. As strict as Brady was, Ava needed to find that balance. Quickly.

Before she ended up running from the past her entire life, like Caley.

"Is that so?" Max ambled toward them from the

fridge, juggling several bottles of water. The look on his face changed from surprise to amusement. "A firewoman."

"It's *firefighter,* like anyone else. And if you're thinking of a cracking a sexist joke, I've heard them all." Caley twirled a colored pencil between her fingers, trying to downplay her irritation.

Max's cheeky smile widened as the back door opened. "Does Brady know?"

"Know what?" Brady stepped inside with an easy smile, his eyes darting from her to Ava to Max. "And where's that water, man?"

"We were just discussing Caley's career." Max slapped a water bottle against Brady's chest as he joined him at the back door. Then he looped his arm around Brady's shoulders, eyes twinkling with mischief. "I think you'll be especially interested in this one. Turns out your temporary nanny is even more of an—" he let out a dramatic cough "—influence than you thought."

"What career?" Confusion dotted Brady's expression as he shoved Max's arm off his back. "Caley doesn't have a job. That's why she was able to babysit Ava. At least, for now anyway." He turned to Caley with a frown. "Right?"

Her heart stammered in her chest as she glanced from Max to Brady. He definitely didn't know about the fire department, but just because it had never come up. She had the sudden feeling it was going to matter. A lot. A storm cloud brewed overhead in the kitchen, tension in the air as static as electricity. She opened her mouth to answer, but Ava beat her to it.

"Dad, don't be silly. Caley has an awesome job. Or she will, at least." Ava hopped up from her chair and carried her new drawing to her dad. "See?"

She could barely make out Ava's picture from her angle at the table, but the outline of the fire truck and water hose through the thin paper was clear enough.

And by the way Brady's face paled, it was plenty clear to him, too.

Chapter Nine

So much for timing.

Brady hammered a wooden post, freshly strung with barbed wire, into the ground with a sharp bang of his hammer. *Bam*. The echoing thud numbed his ears and sent a tingle down the hand he'd used to brace against the post, but unfortunately the physical labor did nothing to erase what had just happened.

Caley. A firefighter.

The woman he hired to be a good influence on his daughter.

The woman he'd almost asked to become an even closer part of his life.

Bam.

Talk about being a bad judge of character. Suddenly, her sitting on her roof to stargaze or wanting to help him round up Spitfire wasn't an issue. Those actions he could justify, could rationalize away with her having a romantic or protective streak.

Firefighting wasn't a streak. It was a choice—a daily choice to put one's life on the line for others. A premade decision to run into the flames when others ran out. It put risk taking on the map in a way a roof and a bull never could.

Bam.

He didn't know if the relief or disappointment was greater: relief that he'd dodged that bullet before he'd actually asked her out on a date or disappointment that now he never could.

Bam.

On second thought, the disappointment was definitely greater. He'd already pictured them at dinner, enjoying a medium-rare steak and him teasing her about her cooking abilities. Laughing at something she said Ava had done the night before. Sharing more of his past with her.

Kissing her good-night at her doorstep.

Bam. The hammer almost hit his thumb that time, so Brady dropped the tool in the grass.

And Ava—he wrenched his work gloves from his hands, pausing to wipe his forehead with the back of one before tossing it on the ground, too. She was already impressed with Caley—thought she hung the moon along with those little glow-in-the-dark stars they'd finally stuck to her bedroom ceiling. Just one more way Caley had stepped in and kept a promise he'd broken. No wonder Ava preferred her—they could talk. They had things in common. Caley was there for her when he couldn't be. He'd be sucked in, too. In fact, he *had* been. Everything about Caley was contagious.

But how far would her influence spread? Would Ava get so caught up in the adventure of Caley's career choice that she'd want to pursue it, too? Or something else equally dangerous? He couldn't lose his daughter. He realized he couldn't put her in a protective bubble all her life, either, but some things *were* in his control.

And he wasn't about to let go of them now.

He slowly picked up the hammer, turning it over in his hands and running his finger over the smooth metal head. The answer was clear, but knowing that truth didn't make it any easier to admit.

Caley had to go.

For all their sakes.

He stared out over his fields, serene and golden in the setting sun.

But maybe mostly for his.

Autumn leaves crunched under her feet as Caley walked through the pasture toward Brady. She flinched at his sharp, jerky movements as he tossed first his hammer and then his gloves onto the ground. Good thing she'd left Ava in the house to finish one last picture for Nonie tomorrow. The last thing Ava needed was to see her dad up in arms—over Caley, no less. She had the feeling Ava's loyalty wasn't exactly in the right place at the moment, and the younger girl would side with her instead.

But with the way Brady buried himself in his work, how could anyone blame her?

Several yards away, Brady tugged his gloves back on and resumed his work. Muscles bunched under the sweat-stained back of his white undershirt as he tugged more fencing into place. His tan work shirt lay rumpled in the grass, as if it, too, were a casualty of whatever war he fought inside his head.

Caley slowed as she neared, partially because she was unsure what to say and partially because she couldn't help but enjoy the view of his labor. She rolled in her lower lip, berating herself. How could she possibly be concerned about an attraction right now, when the man had all but run out of the house at the news of her career?

Maybe she should go back to the house. Give him space to think. Apparently her being a firefighter was a big deal—but why couldn't he just talk to her? Surely he wasn't one of those old-fashioned, sexist types who thought women belonged in the kitchen. Then again, wasn't that how he treated Ava?

No, she wasn't ready for this conversation after all. Not when her pulse leaped just from watching the man work. She needed to get her reactions under control before she let herself get hurt. Before she let herself feel something that would get them all in trouble. She needed time to put her armor in place—the armor that had somehow slipped when she crossed the county line into Broken Bend, and had yet to right itself.

A thin branch snapped under her feet, and Brady threw a look over his shoulder as he straightened.

So much for going back to the house. His intense gaze drew her in, raking down the length of her before meeting her eyes.

And blinking her away.

Just like that, he went back to the fence in his hands. Was that an invitation to stay, or a demand to leave? Indignation began a steady burn in her stomach. This might be his land and his house, but if he wouldn't even dignify her with words, then she'd make her own decisions.

"Who do you think you are?" The words flew from her lips before she could censor them as she closed the distance toward him.

He dropped the fencing again, his gloved hands landing on his jeans-clad hips as he turned to face her. He didn't look surprised, as if he knew even before she did that she'd come for a fight. "It's not who I am. It's who you are."

"Let me guess. A female firefighter." She crossed her arms over her chest, her heartbeat accosting her ears.

"No. A firefighter."

"Don't pretend like the adjective doesn't matter."

Brady tugged off his gloves again but didn't throw them this time, despite the frustration seeping from his expression. "It's not about being a woman."

She hitched her eyebrows at him, and his concentrated stare broke away. "Right. Just like I thought. It's always about being a woman." She'd heard it all before, men backpedaling when she confronted them about their old-fashioned, misguided beliefs. She hadn't made it this far to be called naive now. She knew how the world worked.

"I don't care in general. I care—" He let out a sigh, before crossing his arms to match her own defensive posture. "I care about my family. I care about the effect it has on Ava."

"You think because her *temporary* nanny is trying to get on the local fire department that she'll be ruined for life?" She let out a huff of disbelief. "If anything is going to ruin her it's—" She bit her own lip to stop the word *you* from escaping.

But from the shock wave of hurt radiating from Brady's face, he heard it anyway.

The wind kicked up, stirring the dry leaves at

their feet and illuminating the silence pulsing between them. One oak leaf, stained crimson and
gold, fluttered in a slow circle before settling on
Brady's boot. He slowly reached down to pick it
up, twirling the short stem between his fingers and
avoiding her eyes. Good. Maybe he wouldn't see
the shame creeping up her neck, the same color
as the leaf. She'd gone too far. He'd apologized in
the past to her. Now it was her turn.

She licked her dry lips. "Brady, I'm sorry, I—"

"No. You're right." The resignation in his voice
cut deeper than any preconceived notions he might
have about women. "I'm doing my best with Ava.
But it's not enough."

"You're doing fine." The protest sounded piti-
ful and weak even to her own ears, and she suddenly wished she could fly away on the wind like
the leaves around them. She shouldn't have come
out here.

Maybe shouldn't have moved here.

"Look. We both know the truth." Brady dropped
the leaf he held and it fell to the ground, missing the previous current of air. Caley stared at it,
mixed among the dry grass and skeletal remains
of other leaves, much less glorious in color. "Ava
might respect me, might love me out of obliga-
tion for the time being. But she doesn't need me."

She snapped her head up to meet Brady's pain-
stricken eyes. "That's not true."

"She needs you." The words grunted from his throat, rough and gravelly. "She needs a woman." He coughed, and when he spoke again, his tone relaxed as if with resignation. "Five minutes ago, I was ready to fire you. But if you leave, she has no babysitter. And I have no cook or housekeeper."

This was it. Her ticket out. She could walk right now. Leave Brady and the annoying chemistry between them and his drama far behind. Leave his old-fashioned tendencies and overprotective streak that brought back memories she desperately wanted to keep buried. But she had to have a paycheck until the fire department came around.

And she had to show Brady that he was wrong. Ava *did* need him—just not the way he was providing. Caley had gone overseas with the Peace Corps and helped poverty-stricken nations, but what good was that if she couldn't help her own neighbors? If she didn't mend that fence and show Brady and Ava the way back to each other, she would have failed at the same mission in her life.

Twice.

She clenched her fists at her side and took a deep breath. Hopefully she—and Brady—wouldn't regret this. She swallowed hard before speaking. "I'd like to keep the job."

"Then we need a truce." He held out his hand to shake hers. "No playing up the fire department in Ava's eyes. No crazy stuff—like roof climbing or bull chasing."

Caley rolled her eyes. "Do you really think I'd put Ava on the roof?"

"I don't know what you'd do." His eyes searched hers, hand outstretched in an offering. "I don't know you."

That burned more than it should have.

"Miss Caley!"

Ava's excited shout made them both turn toward the house. She stood framed in the open back door, waving something wildly over her head. "Your pager just went off!"

Of all the timing. Caley turned back to Brady just in time to see him withdraw his hand.

"Duty calls." His lips thinned into a tight line and he swiveled toward his fence.

"My duty is with your daughter when I'm here." Caley grabbed at his arm, his sun-warmed skin heating her palm like a branding iron. She dropped her hand to her side, noting the way Brady's eyes darted to his arm as if he'd been burned. Chemistry or not, she had something to say. And he needed to hear it. "My volunteer work is strictly after babysitting hours. You need to know that." She kept her promises. She would do right by Ava—that was her first priority. Didn't he see that? *I don't know you.* The pain shook her deeper than she'd expected. They'd had a connection. On the roof of her house. In the bed of his truck. In the kitchen, surrounded by broken glass. How could he say that?

"But what about when the job is over?" Brady removed his hat and ran his hand through his hair, sweeping the dark strands over his head before securing the brim back in place. "What then?"

"What's it matter to you?" She swallowed the hurt she couldn't tame. "Then I'll just be a *female* firefighter." She strode away before he could answer.

And more importantly, before she could figure out why tears burned the backs of her eyes.

Chapter Ten

❧

Of all the places a child could be on a Saturday morning, Ava seemed perfectly content to relax by Nonie's bedside, playing Go Fish with a crinkled deck of cards and arguing over which game-show rerun to watch on TV.

Caley was jealous of a ten-year-old.

She shifted in her hard chair, the vinyl seat chilly through her capri pants, and shivered. The nursing home must keep the thermostat on fifty degrees, but Nonie didn't seem to notice, even wearing a thin flowered housedress. The flow from the air vents rustled the pictures Ava had colored on the bulletin board by Nonie's bed. She and Ava had been there for almost an hour already, and neither her grandmother nor the younger girl cared about the cold. They were having too much fun.

While Caley watched from the sidelines, alternating between mentally replaying her conversation with Brady from the evening before—and wondering what on earth she'd thought coming back to Broken Bend would actually accomplish. She wasn't cheering her grandmother up, a near stranger was. Nonie didn't need her now any more than she had when Caley left home at the age of eighteen, determined to make her own way in the world.

And shake off the proverbial leash her father had fixed on her.

Nonie slapped a card on top of the rolling bedside table. "Eight matches! I win again."

"Next time we're playing to ten." Ava frowned as she gathered up the cards and stacked them into a pile. "Or twelve."

Nonie puckered her lips, bright red with lipstick today. "Bring it, little missy. I'm not afraid of you."

Ava giggled. "I've got to use the restroom." She hopped off the foot of the bed and headed into the adjoining bathroom, then popped her head around the frame and shook a warning finger at Nonie. "Don't cheat."

Nonie threw her head back and laughed as the bathroom door clicked shut.

"Ava." Caley shook her head in embarrassment. "She was kidding. I hope."

"She's a good kid. Let her have her fun—besides, I can't say the thought hadn't crossed my mind in the first place." Nonie turned her still-twinkling gaze on Caley. "Want me to deal you in?"

Caley slid her hands under her thighs, her finger finding a tear in the vinyl and rubbing the exposed padding. With their ten-year-old buffer no longer in the room, tension crept into the vacant places between them. "No, thanks." She swiped her hair out of her face, ruffled by the air-conditioning vent over her head. "I was never very good at card games."

"You don't have to be good at something to do it." Nonie shuffled the cards with bony, blue-veined fingers, her eyes never leaving Caley's. "Didn't I teach you that much?"

She swallowed hard. "You taught me a lot, Nonie." Too bad so much of it was in hindsight. Still, the pain of the not-so-distant past lingered deep. Her mother had left. Her father had outright rejected her.

And Nonie had stayed silent.

Of all three, that might hurt the worst.

Her eyes darted to the drawings Ava had created, and once again she longed for the days when she could express herself through a crayon and earn her grandmother's favor so easily. Looking back, her pictures hadn't been very impressive. She still couldn't draw or paint to save her life, despite signing up for lessons as a young adult.

But Nonie had always made her feel talented and important. Worthwhile. She'd always managed to offset the abandonment Caley fought after her mom traded her relationship with her dad for a man with a thicker wallet; to offset the way her father made her feel—stifled. Incapable. Useless. Somehow, her grandmother had kept those precarious scales balanced.

Until Caley left.

"So, my dear—are you ever going to talk about it?" Nonie began dealing out the cards for the Go Fish pond in the center of the table.

Caley focused on the game-show contestant leaping excitedly around a lit stage on the TV, almost unable to speak around the lump in her throat. "Talk about what?" There she went with denial again, but the contrary required too much of her. Not now. Not yet.

"That elephant sitting right there." Nonie gestured with her gray-streaked head to the empty far corner of the room.

She smiled despite herself. She'd missed that humor. Old age and disease might be slowly ravaging her grandma's body, but they weren't taking her wit. Or her heart. But the past was still written—and that elephant had a name. One she wasn't ready to bring up.

Nonie finished handing out the cards, then lay back against her propped pillow. "So I take it you're out of the Peace Corps?" The change of subject came quickly. Her grandmother had always been able to read her. The fact that Nonie knew not to push the previous topic just made her all the more endearing—and heaped an extra layer of guilt onto Caley's already weary shoulders.

She nodded slowly, licking her suddenly dry lips. "I did a stint in Guam for a year before college." She'd invited both Nonie and her dad to her graduation at Baylor University, but they hadn't come. She pushed forward, trying not to let the negative invade what could be a positive conversation—their first since her arrival in Broken Bend. "I've been a firefighter the past several years, and an EMT."

Nonie's eager nod bolstered her courage—that, and her grandmother's lack of surprise over the not-so-typical career choice. Then again, Nonie had always believed in her. That was part of why it hurt so badly that she hadn't shown her support when it mattered the most.

"So what's next?" Nonie tilted her head with genuine interest.

"I'm thinking about becoming a paramedic soon." She lifted one shoulder in a shrug. "But it just depends."

"On what?"

Inside the bathroom, the toilet flushed. Their moment of private conversation was coming to an end, and she didn't know if she felt disappointed or relieved. "Right now it depends on the local fire department and if they hire me soon." She hesitated, hating the taste of truth on her tongue. But it had to be said. "And on how long I stay."

The applause from the show on the television suddenly sounded louder than the fire alarms at the station. Nonie's eyes narrowed, and her red-stained lips pursed once again. But not in judgment. In understanding. "You know, elephants don't just leave of their own will. They set up camp and eat peanuts until you kick them out."

"I know." Emotion burned her throat and she coughed against it. Inside the bathroom, water ran in the sink. Ava would be out any minute. But she had one more question, one that plagued her every night whether she was in her own bed, a fire department cot or a sleeping bag under the stars. "Is it too late, Nonie?"

Her grandmother's face softened, the wrinkles around her eyes relaxing into a satisfied smile. "No, my dear. It's never too late to come home."

That should be the last fence that needed mending. And if it wasn't, well—he might just have to hope the cows came back if they got out again. How much barbed wire could a man pull in a single week?

Brady rotated his sore shoulder, then wiped

sweat off his brow as he studied the grassy landscape, burned yellow in the autumn sun and heat.
After an especially hard day's work, nothing
brought more peace and contentment than viewing his rolling acres of land—land that had been
in his family for generations. Land he toiled over
to support his family, to leave a legacy. One day
all of this would be Ava's.

The thought left him strangely unsettled. Brady
took in the curve of the horizon, reality pressing
hard upon his chest as he packed his tools in the
saddlebags dangling from Nugget's tack. Unlike
training up a son to take over the family business,
he hadn't done that with Ava. She wouldn't have a
clue how to run a ranch once he was gone. She'd
probably have to sell the property, and there went
his family's century of blood and sweat. But what
choice did he have?

His mood darker than before, Brady fought the
hopelessness rising up his throat. He tightened the
straps of his bag harder than necessary, the jerk
sending Nugget sidestepping. If only he'd said no
when Jessica insisted on riding that stubborn horse
he'd used to own. If only he'd seen the warning
signs, been closer when the stallion flattened his
ears and snorted. If only he'd caught her. Would
they have a son by now, if it had gone differently?
Would he be less uptight about Ava—the only
blood he had left?

Would he have ever discovered what it meant to have a happy marriage?

But as his grandfather used to say when Brady was growing up, if wishes were horses, they'd all be swatting flies.

He mounted Nugget just as the horse lifted his head and pricked his ears toward the north. A slow-moving blob crested the hill from the direction of the house, and Brady frowned. Unless Max had doubled in size since he saw him at lunch, it wasn't his friend approaching him on horseback.

He clicked his tongue at Nugget, and the horse obediently moved forward, blowing through his nose. He recognized the other rider's mount. In fact, Brady did, too. The black-and-white patches belonged to his retired quarter horse, Penny. The docile mare was older than dirt and had long since paid her dues, earning a retirement in the pasture. He rode her every now and then for exercise or when Nugget was lame, but Max never did. What was going on?

Penny drew closer and Brady abruptly pulled back on Nugget's reins. The blob wasn't one large person. It was two smaller ones—Caley and Ava. And Scooter trotted right along beside them, tongue lolling happily from his mouth.

Brady pressed his lips together until they hurt, waiting until the unlikely threesome rode up beside him before he spoke. Ava sat behind the saddle, holding on to Caley with both arms while two full saddlebags dangled by their legs.

Despite Caley's apparent ease on horseback, he couldn't stop the fear—and frustration—beginning to boil in his stomach. How dare Caley put his kid on a horse and ride out to the back pastures without asking him first? And after the talk they just had last night? She was either completely dense, or was pushing her boundaries with him to see how far she could go. Neither option sat well with him. The slow boil began churning into a cauldron of emotion. And Ava—she knew she wasn't allowed to ride. What was she thinking?

Then he took one look at Caley's glowing expression and Ava's eyes, lit with excitement, and swallowed the bitter words threatening to burst from his mouth.

"Surprise!" Caley stopped Penny beside Nugget. The two horses butted noses before stretching against their bits to graze the grass at their feet.

"We brought you a picnic." Ava shoved her hair behind her ears, face shining with anticipation. "Chicken salad sandwiches, fruit, chips and cookies. I made the chocolate chip ones this time." She playfully tapped Caley's back, and a light pink burn spread up her cheeks.

"Yes, the cookies are edible this time." Caley rolled her eyes and grinned. "I know it's a light supper, but Ava wanted to surprise you. Wasn't sure how to pack spaghetti in a saddlebag."

They could have driven it out in the truck, for one thing, or waited for him to get home and eaten in the backyard or in the barn.

But Brady had a hard time holding on to his frustration when Caley looked as good as she did in the saddle. So natural. Not like Jessica, who had sat rigidly and clung to the saddle horn as if she'd known what was coming, projecting her fear onto her mount. Caley rode straight and relaxed, her body melding to the saddle, her forearm resting casually against the horn as she gripped the reins firmly in one hand.

"Dad? Is that okay?" Ava's brow furrowed and he realized he'd been staring at Caley instead of responding to their menu.

"Sounds good." Brady tore his eyes from Caley and forced a smile at his daughter. They'd discuss the disobedience part later. "Let's head toward the pond. There's a great flat rock over there that can serve as a table."

Ava squealed with excitement, emitting a bark from Scooter and sending Nugget's head jerking up, grass dangling from his lips. Penny just continued to graze. Poor old girl probably hadn't even heard the high-pitched noise. Of all the horses in his barn, Penny had definitely been the safest choice. But still, no animal was 100 percent trustworthy—and his rules were not supposed to be broken, surprise or no surprise.

He kept a close eye on Ava as they rode side by side toward the pond, and didn't relax until he helped her slide to the ground and she was clear of both horses. He instructed her to set out their dinner while he and Caley settled the horses. She gladly obliged, Scooter at her heels.

"I hope this was okay." Caley lowered her voice to a whisper, following his lead as he looped Nugget's reins around a nearby tree branch. "Max saddled Penny for us. He said you wouldn't care if Ava was on Penny as long as I was riding with her."

Max. Brady let out a slow sigh, wishing he had a way to vent his frustration without letting either of them know. Figured his friend had something to do with this—probably trying to push him further toward Caley. If he didn't back off soon, they would be having a long talk—and not as friends. As boss and employee.

"Ava isn't supposed to ride. Period." Brady stepped back to allow Nugget room to graze, and came to stand beside Caley. Her shorter stature barely met his chin, but her entire presence radiated strength. Capability.

Yet she hadn't lived the nightmare he'd lived. She wasn't a father, or a mom, for that matter. She didn't get it. Firefighters took risks every day. She had no idea whom he'd become because of life. Had no clue what it felt like to walk every day in his boots.

But he refused to be the ogre who rudely pointed it out during a surprise picnic.

"She knows the rules, but thought it was okay because other adults said so." Brady glanced at his daughter, who was humming off tune as she set up their picnic with all the care of a fancy tea party. She straightened the napkins, tilted her head, and straightened them again.

His heart melted a little, and when he looked back at Caley, he knew she'd seen it inside him, too. He ducked his head, but it was too late. Her slim hand rested on his forearm, prickling like he'd brushed up against an electric fence. "She thought of this on her own, Brady. Not to disobey. To surprise you."

Her arm slipped back to her side, and he immediately missed its warmth despite the early-evening sun beating down on his back.

Caley crossed his arms over her chest, looking at Ava though directing her words at him. "She misses you. A girl needs her daddy." Her voice hitched on the last word, and he caught a glimpse of moisture crowding her eyes before she forcefully blinked it away. "Just remember that, okay?"

All thoughts of giving another lecture faded as Caley strode back to Ava, wiping at her eyes and putting on a bright smile as she congratulated Ava on her beautiful place settings.

Brady made his way over to their makeshift table at a slower pace, stomach growling at the sight of the spread before him, arm burning at the memory of Caley's touch.

And heart aching at the truth of her words.

Chapter Eleven

Walking into a church building never held so much potential to start a proverbial fire—and not the kind Caley knew how to put out.

She cast a wary glance around the interior of the church where she'd grown up. Not much had changed—the worn welcome table overflowing with service programs and sign-up sheets still reigned in the corner of the lobby, and the bulletin board of thank-you notes and upcoming events still hung to the left of the back double doors. To her right, people filed into the carpeted sanctuary, where she knew the same cross would still hang over the choir loft—the cross she used to stare at as a child, when she pilfered peppermints from Nonie's purse and tried to figure out if God was any different than her father lounging on the couch back home.

Nope. Nothing had changed at all. What was she doing here?

A tug on her hand reminded her. She glanced down at Ava, who grinned up at her. "I'm so glad you came with us today, Miss Caley." She looked over her shoulder at her dad, who had somehow lagged behind and gotten roped into a conversation on cattle with a man in a starched suit. "Now Dad will have someone to sit with while I'm in children's church."

Panic began a slow crawl up her throat. When she attended church as a child, they didn't offer children's church past first grade. "You mean, you don't come to the main service?" She tried to ignore the burning awareness in her midsection that came with the thought of sitting in a pew next to Brady.

When Ava had asked her last night after their picnic to come to church, she'd reluctantly agreed, not wanting to put a damper on their otherwise successful evening. Brady had backed off the lectures after she reminded him of Ava's fragile feelings, and they'd enjoyed their supper together without further incident. He'd insisted Ava ride back to the house with him on Nugget. Somehow, though, the sight of the girl tucked into her dad's arms more than made up for the lingering evidence of his lack of confidence in Caley. All in all, it'd been a great night that had plenty of potential to carry into a great morning.

She just figured Ava would be sitting between them on the pew.

Since her and Brady's hesitant truce in the pasture two days ago, she felt as though she walked on eggshells—no, make that on a tightrope suspended above eggshells. One false move and she could lose her job, along with her opportunity to make a difference in Ava's life and spare her neighbors the pain she'd endured—still endured. Or at the least, if Brady couldn't fire her because of his own desperate need for a nanny, he could make things beyond awkward for all of them.

Not that Ava and Max weren't accomplishing the same already, with their exaggerated winks and wiggling eyebrows constantly pointing in Caley and Brady's direction. They might as well draw hearts and arrows in the air between them for all their subtlety.

Too bad it didn't matter. She and Brady were worlds apart in all the ways that counted most. He was a small-town rancher, and she was—well, she was anything but Broken Bend. She was here for Nonie, and Nonie alone. When that family duty was fulfilled Caley would be on the road again, where she fit in the best.

Alone.

"They offer kids church here until you're old

enough for the youth group." Ava pushed open the door that led to the Sunday-school wing, and Caley flinched at the loud click of the latch. "Watch out for Dad's singing." Ava giggled. "Uncle Max says it could call a moose from three states away." She waved and ran off to her class.

Great. Talk about rumors getting started about her and Brady. They'd also feed the hope she saw blooming in Ava's heart that there was something between Caley and her dad.

She briefly closed her eyes and drew a deep breath to steady herself, trying to shake off the negative thoughts. Just being in this building made her tense, made her overreact. Made the years of regrets leap from the beige wallpaper and stick to her dress like a name tag. Labeling. Pointing out her flaws. Her guilt.

Making her wonder if she hadn't been right about God all this time after all.

"The service is this way." Brady's warm voice broke through her reverie, and he gestured to the sanctuary, probably assuming she'd never been there before. When he admitted to knowing Nonie back when they first met, she'd never let on that she grew up here and had attended the same church he spoke of. Probably better to play down her history before he picked up any details of her past. For some reason, the thought of Brady thinking badly of her rankled.

She hesitantly followed him inside, the organ's music blending with the congregation's hearty welcome of friends and neighbors. She wasn't either to anyone in this room. Not anymore. She'd seen enough of the furtive glances at her dad's funeral years ago to ensure that any reputation she'd earned here had been covered by a fine black film. A permanent film.

Resisting the urge to wipe her sweaty palms on her sheath dress, Caley slid into a pew near the back beside Brady, thankful he wasn't a front-row kind of guy. She made sure to sit a respectful distance away in a futile effort to curb rumors. It wouldn't matter. The attractive, single rancher sitting in church with the town's most-gossiped-about runaway? Tongues would be wagging, and not in prayer.

Caley squelched the groan rising up her throat and flipped open the hymnal, as if her life depended on finding the right page before the first song began. She carefully kept her eyes averted from the giant wooden cross on the front wall.

"Sorry I got stuck back there," Brady leaned slightly toward her to whisper. "I didn't mean to leave you in the hallway alone. I know it's rough to be in a new place."

She looked up just as he grinned and immediately wished she hadn't.

His breath smelled like peppermints. "Sometimes life is still too much like junior high."

No kidding. She forced a smile she didn't feel, finally finding the correct page number in the book and running her finger down the gold-trimmed pages. "It's not a problem. Ava showed me the ropes." *And then bailed.*

He shifted in the pew, tugging the leg of his stiff jeans over the top of his dress boot. "I've come here for years, but I still feel new at times myself." His thumb tapped an uneasy rhythm on his knee as he scanned the room like a cornered tiger. "We haven't been coming back for long— since my wife's death."

The word *wife* on his lips sent a quiver straight through her stomach and up her spine. She wasn't jealous—was she? That was ridiculous. He and Ava were obviously still handling their grief over the loss, and her place in the middle of that was complicated enough.

"I don't blame you for staying away." The truth slipped out before she could censor it. She rested the hymnal in her lap and quickly fanned herself with her program, wishing the organist would stop the introduction already and start the service.

Brady shot her an inquisitive stare, and she felt the need to clarify despite the fear of shoving her black flats farther into her mouth.

"I just mean it's hard going back to places where

people know everything about you. And want to talk about it when you don't." She shrugged, looking away from his steady gaze lest he figure out they weren't talking about his own past anymore. Her cheeks burned, and she fanned harder.

He opened his mouth to reply, but the service began and the congregation began a rousing chorus she didn't recognize. Probably for the best.

Because despite how everything in the room remained the same, nothing about it felt familiar.

Brady could barely focus on the words of the sermon, so aware was he of Caley next to him. She sat so far away he could have stacked at least two hymnals side by side between them, but still, even that proximity sent a warm sensation prickling down his arms. Her voice rising during the chorus of "Amazing Grace" a few minutes ago, clear as a cowbell ringing over an open pasture, gave him more peace than he'd felt in church in years.

And an uncanny sense of home.

How did she put into words so perfectly what he'd felt all this time? *It's hard going back to places where people know everything about you.* She clearly spoke from experience. Maybe whatever it was that put that thought in her heart was the reason that kept her moving all over the country.

He didn't pray anymore, but if he did, he'd sure

give serious thought to petitioning God about His logic. The first woman Brady had felt something for since Jessica, and she was as untouchable as burrs matted on Wranglers. Max might have thought Caley's career ambitions were amusing, but they changed everything. He refused to let anyone into his and Ava's life that would just leave—be it by choice or accident. Someone who would take unnecessary risks and put themselves repeatedly in harm's way. He couldn't live with himself if he lost anyone else he was responsible for.

He had a hard enough time living now.

Yet despite those truths—he couldn't quite convince his heart to follow his mind's lead.

"…consuming fire."

Brady's head snapped up at Pastor Dave's words. What fire? His chest burned at the realization he'd been completely zoned out, and shot a quick look at Caley. If she'd noticed, she didn't let on. Yet the doodles on her program indicated she might be guilty of the same.

"The book of Hebrews—not to mention the entire Bible—teaches us that God's kingdom can't be shaken." Dave paced the pulpit, the stage lights reflecting off his reading glasses. "It teaches us to be grateful for this fact. For this security." He paused, gazing out at the congregation. "For our God is a consuming fire."

Brady swallowed, averting his eyes to smooth the crease of his jeans. Of all the times to tune back in. Security? Hardly. There was nothing secure about faith. Faith was blind trust. Risky. Dangerous.

No, thanks.

"It teaches us to therefore offer to God acceptable worship—with reverence." Pastor Dave stopped his midstage stroll and lingered at the pulpit, resting his forearms against the wooden structure. "For our God is a consuming fire."

Brady wished he would stop saying that word. What happened to the images of God from Ava's pink Bible—light shining through clouds, a slightly blurred but happy-faced figure on a throne? That was the God he wanted Ava to know right now. A consuming fire—well, he'd nearly been in one before, and there wasn't anything holy about it. It was pure evil.

"Reverence means not only respect, but awe." Pastor Dave's expression gentled as he picked up his Bible from the pulpit. "When was the last time you were in awe of our Lord?"

Brady licked his dry lips, while next to him, Caley started a new drawing of wildflowers. In awe of God? It'd been a while. Maybe forever. He and Jessica started out on the right foot in their marriage. Then their church attendance became hit or miss. She got pregnant right away, and the ranch took up more and more time. Then, when their marriage got rocky, neither of them wanted to fake it at church anymore.

And after her death, well—not much to praise God for after that. Oh, sure, everyone told Brady he was blessed to still have Ava. They were blessed to have their health and the opportunity to start over. But what did that matter when a little girl had lost her mom? When a grown man became buried under the rubble of regret and guilt? When a marriage that had barely even had a chance crumpled entirely?

Where was God in that?

He couldn't do this today. Not with the memories assaulting his soul. Not with Caley's cinnamon scent wafting up his nose and threatening his resolve. Not with the past and the hopelessness of the future tying a double-layered noose around his neck.

In one quick movement, he stood and brushed out of the pew past Caley and through the double doors. He didn't look back. He didn't apologize.

And he didn't stop until he felt wind on his face.

Chapter Twelve

The next several days with Ava flew by, and before Caley knew it, Wednesday afternoon arrived with a blast of muggy heat, more worthy of a midsummer day than autumn. She had the afternoon off since Ava was staying at a friend's house after school, so she decided to stay in and cook Chinese food for herself. Brady had told her not to worry about cooking for just him, that he could heat up a hot dog or make a sandwich easily enough for one.

Thank goodness, because after their awkward conversation in church, she couldn't imagine spending an evening alone with him in his kitchen. Not with the reminder of the broken casserole dish lingering in the corner of her eye every time she stepped foot in the room. Not with their tentative truce filling the unspoken spaces between them. Not when she was dying to find out why he'd left the sanctuary Sunday morning and waited for her and Ava in the parking lot.

Caley set her pager on the kitchen counter in her rental house, where she could easily hear the beep while she cooked supper. So far this week she'd made one volunteer run—a wreck involving a flipped car, an out-of-towner and a particularly unforgiving tree. Thankfully the woman had been all right, but the rush of adrenaline, the urgency to perform well and to save a life, left Caley on a high for days.

She sort of hoped the pager would buzz tonight. Not only did she still need to prove herself to Chief Talbot and get hired, she needed to feel important. Needed to feel needed.

Needed to know her choices all these years had actually been worth it.

She found her trusty wok and began preparing the stir-fry, her mind straying back to Brady and his issues from Sunday. The more she got to know him, the more she realized he was a man of many layers.

And something within him just begged for her to unwrap them all.

She tossed some salt into the skillet and turned up the fire, blinking away her train of thought. Brady was her boss. Ava's dad. Not a romantic interest, no matter how good he'd smelled during church or how her stomach reacted when he'd accidentally brushed his hand across her arm when sliding a hymnal into the book rack. Just because Ava was eager to see them get together didn't make it a good idea. Caley didn't do long-term relationships—mainly because that involved commitment to one spot.

And she wasn't ready to stand still.

Besides, most of the men she'd encountered were too intimidated by her to support her dreams. And she refused to be like her mother and commit to one man, only to leave him high and dry for the next, better offer. If that tendency ran in her genes, well, she had to be extracareful before settling down.

If she ever could.

She brushed at the sizzling vegetables with a spatula, wishing she could get inside Brady's head long enough to know what part of the sermon had prompted him to exit. He'd played it off outside when she and Ava joined him, and she wasn't about to ask in front of his daughter. Not when she'd been none the wiser inside children's church and came out sharing an animated story of Noah's ark.

But it wasn't a sick stomach that had driven Brady from the pew. If Caley had one guess, it'd probably been the same realization that had tempted her to run out, as well.

That God wasn't who they thought He was.

She stabbed at the stir-fry. Admitting the thought should feel like progress—at least, that's what her old counselor would have told her—but somehow it just felt even more disrespectful. Like another strike on her spotty record. There was nothing progressive or productive about realizing the faith of your childhood was stabilized on sand instead of rock. Her shaky structure had toppled the day her father died, with so much left unsaid between them, and it could never be rebuilt. God was like her dad: hard to please. Impossible to understand.

And even harder to see.

Nonie had seen God when Caley was growing up. Still did, even from a nursing home bed. But Caley couldn't reconcile that God with the one in her mind, the one who had allowed her mother to abandon her when she was young and allowed her father to disown her. The one who surely expected better of her than what she had to give. The one who wanted to stifle her instead of help her fly.

The smell of burned onion and green pepper filled her nostrils just as the smoke alarm above her head began to chime. With a start, she turned off the fire, grabbed a pot holder, yanked the burned veggies from the stove top and set them aside. Then she climbed on a chair, stood on tiptoe and stabbed the alarm with the end of her spatula. The incessant beeping mercifully stopped, and she rubbed her ears before returning the chair to the table. So much for supper. That's what she got for being so distracted she nearly burned down her own house. That wouldn't look particularly stellar on her résumé for the district station.

Caley tossed the ruined stir-fry into the trash and ran cold water over the pan before resting it in the sink. Looked like a sandwich night for her, too. Maybe she'd slap together some turkey and mayo and finally hang that picture of the fireman in her living room, try to salvage the evening. Certainly beat thinking about ranchers next door and spiritual impasses.

A sudden knock sounded at the door, and she scrambled to open it, grateful for a distraction from her thoughts.

But no such luck. The object of her reverie stood framed in the doorway, cowboy hat absent and his dark hair mussed as if he'd just run his fingers through it. Her breath caught in her throat, and she absently reached up to smooth her own hair.

"Sorry to bother you on your night off." Brady's tone, borderline professional, sent her hand sliding back to rest aimlessly at her side. "I think this belongs to you." He gestured to the ground, where Scooter sat on top of his boots, tongue lolling to the side.

"Scooter!" Caley bent down and grabbed her dog's collar. He barked happily and licked her face before wrestling free of her grip and darting inside the house. "He must have gotten out. I thought he was still asleep in my room."

"No problem. He showed up on my doorstep, whining and scratching at the glass. You might want to check your back door, though, since this one was locked." Brady took half a step inside and sniffed the air twice. The corners of his lips slowly turned upward. "You were cooking."

His pointed look made his words a statement rather than a question—and that rakish grin made his distant facade fall away. Her stomach fluttered at the attention. Maybe keeping it professional was better after all. Though on second thought, he was making fun of her—again.

She lifted her chin and tried to forget about the chocolate chip cookies. And the broken casserole dish. And the stir-fry carnage in her trash can. "Why, yes, I was."

He sniffed again, stepping far enough into the house that Caley reluctantly shut the door behind him. "And you burned it."

"Why, yes, I did."

He let out a snort, half disbelief and half amusement, and she couldn't help but chuckle, too. "I would say I'm surprised, but..." His voice trailed off and his blue eyes lit as his gaze drew her in. Gone was the stress from church, the bags under his eyes from working long hours. Gone was the shield he threw up every time he stood in her presence. In his eyes lingered nothing but humor, appreciation—and maybe a little something more.

She cleared her throat, determined to keep things light between them despite the electricity pulsing through the air, and offered a sheepish smile. "So, am I fired?" She edged a step toward the kitchen and he followed, as if drawn by a magnet.

"Not yet." His gaze fell to her lips, then quickly away.

She drew a deep breath, then opened the refrigerator door, putting it between them as a shield. "Can I make you a sandwich?"

He settled at a bar stool near the small island and shook his hair out of his eyes. "I don't know. Sounds dangerous."

"Very funny." Caley grabbed a loaf of bread and a package of deli meat from the shelf, and then plucked a bottle of mayo and a jar of pickles from the door. "Even I can't mess this up."

"Actually, I'm sure you could—"

"Watch it, now." She held up both hands in mock defense. "It's not my fault. I'm usually a decent cook. It's just something about—" This time she interrupted herself, biting down on her lip to clamp the rest of her sentence before it could release. Something about *him?* Not the best thing to admit, no matter how true. Not with their understanding between them. Not with her temporary status in Broken Bend, his aversion to her career choices and her aversion to his child-rearing choices all fixed between like an inter-mingling maze of brick walls.

She didn't finish her sentence, and he didn't ask her to. Probably because he saw through the veneer covering her feelings—the feelings that practically screamed her interest in him, and went beyond that of an employee or a caring nanny.

The feelings she better get a lid on before she left more carnage in her wake than burned vegetables.

"I'll take a sandwich." Brady's calm voice slid her train of thought solidly back on track, and she exhaled the overwhelming emotion that had been building. "No mayo."

She slapped together two sandwiches, putting extra mayo on hers just to make him wrinkle his nose at the sight, and slid his across the island on a napkin. "Bon appétit."

He took a big bite, the gleaming light in his eyes suggesting more teasing was about to commence. She spoke first to stop it. "Thanks for bringing Scooter back. I hope he didn't bother you."

"No big deal. At this point, what's one more four-legged creature on a ranch?" He shrugged and wiped his mouth with his napkin. "At least this one isn't about to make more animals." He nudged

Scooter, who had crawled under the island in hope of catching crumbs, playfully with his foot. "I've got an expecting mare and several cows due in the next few weeks—out of season. It wasn't the first time Spitfire's gotten out of his pen."

"Hopefully the last, though." Caley shuddered at the memories of that day. Most were pretty scary—though maybe the one of her lying in Brady's arms in her truck was the most terrifying of all. Did he think about it as much as she did?

She risked a glance at his face, but his expression remained stoic as he continued rattling off facts about his herd. She listened closely, not because the topic was particularly interesting, but because of the intensity with which he spoke. Ranching really was his passion. Why couldn't he see Ava shared that same dream? Why couldn't he respect it if he felt the same?

"Enough about that." Brady finally leaned back with a sigh, hooking his booted feet under the island. "I can ramble on about ranch stuff all day. It's nice talking to someone besides Max about these things. Hard to stop, I guess."

"What, Nugget doesn't give you good advice on baling hay and mending fences?" Caley grinned. "Shocking."

"Sometimes I wonder if he'd give better advice than Max." Brady snorted. "Sorry. I probably shouldn't have said that. We're best friends, but sometimes..." His voice trailed off and he shook his head. "We go way back. Maybe too far."

Caley began to put their condiments back in the refrigerator. "No offense taken. I understand." Though, really, she didn't. She never stayed anywhere long enough to have a permanent best friend. Someone reliable, someone always there. Someone to vent to or even vent about when she was having a bad day, and know it was still all right. What would that feel like?

Brady and Max were a prime example. They obviously argued and drove each other crazy, but worked so well together they took care of entire ranch between the two of them. And Ava clearly adored her "uncle." That spoke a lot for his character, even if his personality rubbed Caley the wrong way.

She peeked at Brady from under her lashes as she returned the mayo jar to the refrigerator door. Talk about opposites. Brady's dark hair and blue eyes were a contrast to Max's lighter brown hair and dark eyes—just like Brady's stoic, steady and resolute manner contrasted with Max's fun-loving, teasing and lighthearted ways.

She'd guess the two of them had been unstoppable in high school.

"So how's Nonie?" Brady capped the lid on the jar of pickles and came around the island to hand them to her.

She slid the jar back on the shelf and wiped the condensation on her jeans. "She's good in so many ways. Mentally, it's as if we're back chatting on her floral-print sofa at her house, like nothing changed. But physically…" She shrugged, not wanting to dwell on the inevitable. "It's a downhill road. She's really weak. More so than I thought at first—apparently she puts on a good front for Ava." After their last visit, she'd watched the strength drain from Nonie as they waved goodbye. Her grandmother had been asleep before they shut the door behind them.

Brady crossed his arms over his chest and leaned back against the sink. "Ava enjoys visiting with her. I'm glad you don't mind letting her tag along."

"Of course. Ava's a good kid. She makes Nonie happy." More than Caley did, but she had to stop thinking like that. Nonie didn't think badly of her, so why should she? Still, the past was hard to let go of. If she opened her heart and set it free, she might break completely. It seemed easier to keep paying for her mistakes. Keep the wall up.

Protect them both from more heartache.

"Speaking of good kids." Caley cleared her throat and nudged the refrigerator door shut with her hip. "You know your daughter is just like you, right?"

Brady's shoulders straightened and he eased slightly upward. "What do you mean?"

"Your love for the ranch. The land. The animals." She turned to face him, wishing she could drill the obvious into his head. "I know it's not really my business, but I can't help but notice how much she longs to be like you. To do what you do."

His lips flattened. "She's a little young."

"She's on the verge of becoming a young woman." Tension knotted in her shoulders, and she crossed her arms, mimicking his defensive posture. "Don't tell me you think women can't run a ranch or take care of livestock. Because I seem to recall saving you from a bull more ornery than y—"

In a flash, Brady stood directly before her, one finger gently covering her lips. "Don't finish that sentence."

The contact of his knuckle, warm against her mouth, sent a spark down her spine. She pressed her lips together, almost distracted from her point.

Almost.

She narrowed her eyes and he dropped his hand to his side but didn't step away. She tried to ignore his proximity and the way her breath hitched in her throat. "Why not?"

"Because you don't mean it. And you'll regret it."

"Regret saying you're ornery? I don't think so."

She meant the words to come out firmly, but they sounded more like flirty banter instead. She licked her lips and stepped back, away from his presence, which did crazy things to her heart—and apparently her capability of speech.

He gave her a dry grin, easing back to the counter where he'd come from and this time hopping up to a seated position on top. His booted feet hung almost to the floor. "I'm not a sexist, Caley. No matter how hard you try to make me that way, it's just not true."

"Maybe not, but you think women don't have any business doing ranch work?" She wanted to plant her hands on her hips but knew how immature the motion would make her look—defeating her point. She clenched her fists at her side in an effort to control the impulse. "Or firefighting?"

His eyes darkened, casting a serious hue back on their conversation. Although that was probably her fault, too. "You don't understand."

"Then enlighten me." They were too far into this to back down now. Besides, Caley had faced bigger giants before and come out victorious. She'd fight for Ava—and herself. Because they deserved it.

And maybe because being angry at Brady was a whole lot easier than trying not to fall for him.

They locked eyes, each daring the other to speak truth first. Caley held his gaze, refusing to blink or look away or admit defeat. She wanted—no, needed—to know his heart on this issue.

Just was too afraid to admit to herself why it mattered so much.

A plethora of emotions flickered through Brady's blue eyes as he clearly debated what to say. Doubt. Hope. Distrust.

Longing.

He was going to cave. She knew it. She could feel it pulsing through the air between them, about to ignite. This was it—the moment she helped him and Ava have a breakthrough. The moment Caley's time on the ranch came to fruition.

The moment she could forget all the reasons why it couldn't work between them and concentrate only on the lingering brand of his finger on her lips.

Beep. Beep. Beep.

Her pager. Caley's heart fell somewhere near the tiled kitchen floor, and she could almost tangibly see the gate between her and Brady slam shut and lock. "Brady, I—"

He just shook his head as she reached across the counter for the black box. How could one little piece of technology have such repeated bad timing? She glimpsed the text scrolling across the tiny screen. Brush fire. Highway 90. All units respond.

She had to go.

He slipped off the counter and headed for the door. "See you tomorrow." He wrenched it open.

She grabbed her purse and keys from the end table and followed him, shoving the pager inside her bag. "Brady, wait." She couldn't stay, couldn't hash it out now. But she couldn't leave with his frustration weighing so heavily on her heart. They'd been close. So close.

He turned abruptly in the open doorway, stopping her short. "Just be careful." His eyes bored into hers, and she couldn't breathe. Could only nod.

He held her gaze a moment longer, then disappeared into the night. She clutched the door frame to regain her balance, inhaling a sharp breath before quickly climbing into her truck and turning over the engine.

She should have taken the frustration as the gift it was. Because the only thing weighing on her now was not the anger she'd expected to see in his eyes.

It was the sadness.

Chapter Thirteen

She'd made it home safely last night—he knew because he stayed up watching until her truck headlights beamed down her driveway at 11:32 p.m.

Brady yawned, almost covering his mouth with his gloved hand before remembering what he'd been doing for the past twenty minutes—mucking out stalls. He'd spent the first half of the night worrying about her, and the second half reliving their argument in her kitchen. He'd been about half a second from telling her the truth about Jessica, from opening up and sharing details he hadn't shared with anyone other than Max, until that pager chimed. Those simple, high-pitched tones managed to serve as a timely reminder that he had no business sharing anything with Caley. Not when she was bound to leave eventually. Not when her career choice might as well stand as an impenetrable wall between them. Not when he needed the exact opposite in a future wife and stepmother for his daughter.

He stabbed the pile of hay harder with his pitchfork. The phrase *life wasn't fair* was perhaps the understatement of the century. What were the odds of him falling for a woman as complicated as Caley Foster after all these years? If only she could have been what she'd seemed when she first moved into the rental house. Sweet. Responsible. Mature.

To be honest, she *was* all of those things.

She was just also so much more.

"For someone who's so attracted to his nanny, you sure don't spend much time inside the house." Max's head popped over the top of the stall next door, where he'd been repairing a loose board.

Brady stopped shoveling and narrowed his eyes. "For someone who's paid to work, you sure don't seem to remember who cuts your check."

"Ouch. Touch a nerve, much?" Max hung his arms over the top of the stall. Sweat beaded on his forehead and he swiped at it with one sleeve, grinning.

"You know how I feel about Caley—and her career. Subject closed." Too bad he couldn't convince himself of the same. But it had to be this way. He wouldn't put himself into a relationship with that level of risk to his—or Ava's—heart again. Nor could he start a relationship where he wanted to change the other person from the get-go. He and Jessica were proof enough of how that method never worked. Opposites might attract initially, but they didn't make for an easy marriage. He wouldn't go that route again.

No, if he ever remarried—and that was a Texas-sized *if*—it'd be to someone who would understand his desires to raise Ava a certain way and not push him to change his opinions. Someone who wouldn't try to force him to explain him choices, but rather step back and respect them.

Now if he could just get Caley's energy, zest and bright-eyed smile out of his head...

Max held up both hands in exaggerated surrender, the hammer tucked between his thumb and forefinger. "Whatever you say. You're the boss."

He went back to whistling under his breath, and Brady had half a mind to switch chores with him. See how feisty his friend felt with pitchfork in hand instead of hammer. But he dutifully continued shoveling. It wasn't Max's fault he'd fought with Caley—again—and been reminded of her choices again. It was his own fault for staying up late and worrying about her as if she was his responsibility. She was hired help. He didn't worry about Max in his off hours, and they were best friends. So what did that say about his feelings toward Caley?

Trouble, was what it spelled. In big, capital letters.

He finally tuned in to what Max was whistling—the old schoolyard song about kissing in a tree. "Cut it out, man."

Max's laughter rang between hammer blows. "Oh, come on, it's a little funny."

Brady hefted his pitchfork into another pile. "Keep your day job." He thought about adding a threat about how Max might not have a chance if he kept it up for long, but he knew it'd fall flat. He'd never fire his best friend, and Max knew it. Max had been there for him through the rough months after Jessica's death, and deep down, he knew his friend just wanted him to find happiness again. Couldn't fault a man for caring.

He might tattoo the word *decorum* across his forehead, though.

Footsteps pounded down the barn aisle. Brady looked up from the stall just as Ava appeared before him, breathless and red-cheeked. Scooter followed at her heels, tongue dripping on the barn floor. He must have followed her from the bus stop near Caley's house. She dropped her denim backpack at her feet, raising a small cloud of hay and dust. "Hey, Dad. Need some help?"

In the barn, with restless horses roaming the pasture right outside, waiting for their stalls to be cleaned and eager for their supper? Not a chance. "I've got it handled, honey."

The hope faded from her eyes, and she stretched on tiptoe to peer over the stall door, Scooter pushing against her legs. "Is that your last one?"

"Two left." Brady checked to make sure none of the horses had wandered back into the barn before resuming his mucking. "How was school?"

Ava ignored him. "Uncle Max, do you need help?" Renewed enthusiasm filled her voice, and Brady fought back a wave of jealousy. She'd always had a bond with his friend. First Max and now Caley. Even Nonie. Would Ava always prefer other adults to him?

Max set down his hammer with a bang and exited the barn door, brushing his hands on his jeans. "Need help? You know what, I think I just might—"

Brady loudly cleared his throat, and Max shot him a look before turning back to Ava. "I mean, I don't right now, darling. Sorry. We're about done here." He looked up and down the barn aisle, his voice rising with interest. "Where's Caley?"

"*Miss* Caley," Brady corrected. He finished filling the wheelbarrow and backed it out into the aisle. Ava gave him a wide berth with a wrinkled nose. See—young girls didn't need to be doing farm chores, anyway. She should be in the house with Caley, cooking. Well, that was probably asking a lot on Caley's watch, but certainly doing art projects or playing in her room. Girl stuff. Safe stuff.

Ava shrugged. "She's in the house, I guess. I just got home from school."

"You didn't go straight inside?" Brady's grip tightened on the wheelbarrow handles. "Ava, you know the rules. You get off the bus and head into the house first thing. Miss Caley might be worried about you. She knows you get home at a certain time."

Her lip pouted slightly. "I just wanted to see you."

The admission tore at his heart, but rules were rules. And his were meant to keep her not only on a routine, but alive. She didn't belong in the barn, not when he was too busy to keep a close eye on her and protect her. It only took a second for his life to unravel. He'd watched it play out before, and he wasn't about to start plucking at loose threads now. "I'm glad you wanted to see me, but—"

"No, you're not." Ava grabbed her backpack from the floor and hitched it on her shoulder, voice warbling with either unshed tears or anger—he couldn't tell which. "You could care less as long as your precious *work* gets done."

He opened his mouth to counter, but a shout from Caley interrupted. "Ava! Are you outside?" Her tone, muffled from the back door, carried a slight note of worry. "Ava!"

Scooter barked and darted out of the barn. Ava darted a glance at Brady, her wary eyes likely expecting an *I told you so*. "Don't worry, I'm going. I'll get out of your way."

Then she ran down the barn aisle toward the house before Brady could say a word.

"I know it hurts your feelings, Ava, but he's your dad." Caley stacked two cookies—store-bought—into a mini tower in front of Ava and slid a glass of milk across the kitchen table toward her. Outside, Scooter whined and pawed at the door. She eyed him, debating breaking Brady's rule about pets in the house and letting him in anyway. He wouldn't go home, almost as though he was worried about Ava after seeing her cry. But that wouldn't be the best example during her impromptu "your dad isn't your enemy" speech.

Caley took a sip of her own milk before continuing. "He's trying to do what's best for you." The words reluctantly escaped through gritted teeth. She'd heard Nonie tell her the same thing growing up over the years—and she hadn't received them any better than Ava appeared to be.

Ava spoke around a big bite of chocolate cookie, crumbs spraying from her lips onto the table. "I don't get it. I'm not going to get trampled because I'm just standing in the barn." She rolled her eyes in true preteen fashion. "I'm the only kid in Broken Bend who has to beg their dad to muck out a horse stall. And still gets told no."

If Ava's situation wasn't so painfully similar to her own childhood, it'd be humorous. She'd never had to beg her dad to let her do chores, but she could relate to Ava's desire for connection, for quality time—and being denied. Her father had chosen fishing and hunting and any other male-dominated hobby over time with her every chance he got—and refused to take her along. If he thought it was dangerous to take her hunting, then why didn't he stay behind and do something else with her instead?

Eventually, her thirsty need for his acceptance and approval morphed into seeking any means of attention—even the negative. Thankfully, her rebellious streak got cut short when she found her passion, the Peace Corps. She'd had to straighten up to make that dream a reality.

But even that noble goal hadn't been worthy of her dad's approval. He'd wanted her to stay in Broken Bend, go to a nearby community college and live at home. But why? To keep her around? To keep control? A little too late for that.

Now it was forever too late.

She didn't want Ava to learn that the hard way. Didn't want this sweet girl to have a life of regrets and failed second chances. Not when Caley was sitting in front of her with the option to guide her otherwise.

Even if she did want to smack some sense into

Brady for being so clueless about his daughter's real needs. Kids needed a roof over their heads, money in the bank and food on the table, but they also needed a whole lot more than that. Right now, she couldn't do much about Brady's side of things. But maybe she could help Ava adjust.

She chose her next words carefully. "Ava, your dad has rules to protect you." She took a deep breath. "My dad was really strict with me growing up, too. I see now that I'm an adult that it's hard for single parents—especially dads—to raise a daughter alone." She reached across the table and briefly patted Ava's arm. "He's doing the best he can."

"I guess so." Ava twisted her second cookie apart and scraped the cream off with her teeth. Chocolate stuck to her bottom teeth when she grinned wistfully. "I wish you were here all the time, Miss Caley. You'd make a great mom."

Something warm and maternal seeped across Caley's stomach. No one had ever told her that before. But then again, she'd always been so busy, moving so quickly, trying to stay one step ahead of her past, that it was hard to show anyone that side of her. In fact, she hadn't even been sure it existed. Kind of difficult to think about future children when she couldn't even determine if she had it in her to stay with one man forever.

Brady was the first man who had ever even

tempted her to consider it. But attraction or not, they were different in too many ways to make it work. She couldn't marry a man who was like her father in all the areas she fought the most. Talk about a recipe for disaster. If her mom had left her dad over money, how could Caley be guaranteed she wouldn't do worse one day?

Even if Ava would make the world's best step-daughter.

She brushed their crumbs off the table and into a napkin. If she looked the girl in the eye, she might tear up. "Your dad loves you, Ava, and it's important that you respect his rules. Even when they don't make sense to you." She swallowed the knot rising in her throat and tossed the napkin into the trash can. If she had listened to Nonie tell her the same thing about ten years ago, would it have made a difference? Could her relationship with her dad been redeemed? She'd never know now. But she could try to encourage Ava. "You already are a great daughter."

"Thanks." Ava took a long sip of milk and then sighed. "I just wish Dad thought that, too."

Caley recognized the sound of that particular heartbreak, and a sudden urgency filled her soul. She sat back down and reached across the table for Ava's hand. This wasn't enough. She was here for a reason, and somehow, she'd find a way to ful-fill her purpose at the Double C ranch. "Listen. I want to help you and your dad figure this out. But we're going to have to take it one step at a time." She held up a warning finger at the hope lighting in Ava's eyes. "That doesn't mean disobeying. It means finding compromises."

"That sounds good." Ava's fingers tightened against hers and she leaned forward with new-found eagerness. "Like more horseback-ride picnics?"

Caley winced. "No. No more of those."

Ava's lips twisted to the side and she pulled her hands away in defeat. "I understand."

"It might even mean making efforts that don't seem that fun at first—like keeping your room clean." Caley rushed forward before Ava's pout fully developed. "Trust me, showing your dad that you can be responsible and mature is the biggest step toward getting what you want."

"It is?" Ava's thin eyebrows shot up her fore-head, and she ran one finger around the rim of her glass. Her eyes narrowed in thought. "How so?"

"You want more responsibility, right? Outside on the ranch and with the animals?" Caley waited for Ava's nod. "Then you have to show him you can be responsible—consistently responsible—with what you're already in charge of. Like cleaning your room, and maybe taking some responsibility with Scooter." She gestured to the back door, where Scooter had finally given up requesting entrance and lain on the outside mat. "And maybe one night this week you could cook your dad supper. Show him that you're growing up. Things like that."

Ava slowly nodded, a grin sliding up her cheeks. "Show him I'm growing up. I like the sound of that. You've got a deal."

They shook on it, and Caley's heartbeat quickened in her chest. She was making a hefty promise, but she'd find a way to keep it. She was doing the right thing—for Ava. For Brady. And even for herself. Repairing what was broken between the two of them wouldn't bring back her dad.

But maybe, when it was time to go, it would help the leaving part hurt a little less.

Chapter Fourteen

Caley knocked on Nonie's open door before entering the room, balancing in her free hand a plate of sugar cookies Ava had whipped up last night after their talk. The cool air inside nearly knocked her backward like always, and she fought a shiver. "Good morning, Nonie."

Her grandmother slowly turned from where she'd been gazing out the window, her curly hair matted against her pillow. She blinked a few times before rubbing her eyes with the back of her gnarled hand.

"I brought you some cookies." Caley set the plate on the bedside table, unable to meet her grandmother's steady gaze. She hated how tired her grandmother looked. Usually when she and Ava came to visit, it was in the afternoon after school. Nonie had been refreshed from a nap and smiled with recently applied lipstick, ready to blast them with her sarcastic wit and pretend to cheat at Go Fish.

But first-thing-in-the-morning Nonie just seemed wilted. Like a stranger, not the woman who helped raised her. It was disconcerting.

Nonie pushed the button that raised the back of the bed and spoke over the slight whirring noise that filled the quiet room. For once, the TV wasn't playing, interrupting their talks with cheers from contestants or blaring commercials. "Tell me those cookies aren't my secret recipe." Her eyes sparkled with hope as life seemed to seep back into her bones. "You never could quite figure it out, could you?"

There was the Nonie she knew. Caley exhaled slowly as she took the chair beside Nonie's bed, her pager digging into her hip. Thank goodness her grandmother had pepped back up. Or rather, thank God. She closed her eyes briefly. *God, I'm not ready to give her up yet. I still have too much to make up for.* She opened her eyes, wishing she could be sure God cared to hear her prayers. But she knew without a doubt He cared for her grandmother, so that had to count for something. Surely He'd listen to prayers about her.

Caley tapped the wrapped plate with one finger. "Don't worry, these are from Ava. Cut and bake." She'd even let Ava cut the dough herself after a quick lesson on kitchen knife safety.

Nonie reached for the plate, and Caley tempered the automatic urge to ask her if she'd had breakfast first. She was a grown woman. Instead, she plucked a cookie free and handed it to Nonie, then took one for herself. This morning definitely deserved sugary comfort. Amazing how awkward it felt already between them without Ava as a buffer.

"So where's my little card buddy today?" Nonie asked, as if reading her mind. She took a bite of cookie and nodded at it. "Not bad for cut and bake. She did good."

"Ava's at school." Caley finished her so-called breakfast in two bites. They *were* good. Ava had baked them to perfection, even if she hadn't actually mixed up the batter. She'd made them in an effort to show her dad responsibility, but unfortunately, Brady hadn't noticed. Or at least hadn't by the time Caley went home.

"I thought it was Saturday." Nonie frowned at the calendar on the nightstand.

"It's Friday." She brushed a sprinkle from the corner of her mouth, unsure what else to say. Was the confusion a simple mistake or a sign that Nonie's sharp mind was slipping after all? Either way, it served as a reminder for Caley that time was short. She rubbed her hands down her pant legs and took a deep breath. "Nonie, you know that elephant that likes hanging out in your room?"

Nonie set her cookie down, only half-eaten, and

raised her bed a few more notches. Her wise eyes narrowed as her gaze drew Caley in. "I was about ready to name him."

"Don't get attached yet." She fiddled with a loose thread on her jeans before clasping her hands in her lap. No more fiddling. No more averting. Just honesty.

Even if her stomach had knotted up like a Boy Scout's practice rope.

She inhaled. "Nonie, I need to apologize."

"For what? Always forgetting that my secret recipe includes coconut oil?" Nonie gestured to the plate of cookies and winked.

The knot in her stomach unraveled an inch. She relaxed slightly for the first time since stepping into the room. "For leaving Broken Bend. I mean, I don't regret the choice, but it was too fast. And the fight with Dad after, well…" She fingered a spot on her jeans before forcing herself to meet Nonie's eyes. "I just wanted out."

"I know you did, honey. And I didn't blame you for that." Nonie adjusted the thin blanket over her legs as she shifted to face Caley. "Small towns can suffocate. They're not meant for everyone." She paused, her eyes searching Caley's. "The way you left is what hurt your father."

"Hurt *him?*" Her back straightened, every nerve on high alert. "I was eighteen—legally an adult. I told him my plans and carried them out. It wasn't my fault he wanted to keep me under his control forever." She knew the words sounded immature leaving her lips, but she couldn't rein them in. This conversation was so long overdue, it was if her teen self had taken over her tongue. "He was the one who abandoned me afterward. Disowned me."

"Abandoned you?" Nonie's penciled eyebrows, smeared from sleep, rose on her wrinkled forehead. "You left Broken Bend, Caley. Not the other way around." She reached for Caley. "We never went anywhere."

She stared at Nonie's pale, blue-veined fingers covering her own tanned ones, then slowly lifted her eyes to meet her gaze. "You didn't come after me." The admission still hurt. The memories. The empty seats at college graduation. The unanswered texts and emails to her dad's phone. Feeling disowned by the family she had left. Her mom had left when she was a child—she'd never thought her dad would follow suit. What made leaving Broken Bend so terrible? What made wanting to make something of herself outside of the county lines an unpardonable sin? It never made sense. Still didn't.

"Caley." Nonie released a heavy sigh as she removed her hand and slumped back against her pillows. "There's a lot here you don't understand." She looked tired again, as if the very conversation drained her of all her remaining energy.

"I understand that I invited you both to my college graduation and neither of you came." Tears burned the back of Caley's eyes. "I admit I expected that from Dad. But not from you."

"What invitation?" Nonie's eyes flashed. "We didn't get an invitation. Not that I saw."

"I mailed it three weeks before the ceremony." She distinctly remembered, even all these years later, clutching the envelope and praying before dropping it down the college campus mail chute. Praying that the invitation would mend fences. Bring her family back. Be the first step toward reconciliation.

Rejected.

"We never got it." Nonie shook her head. "I assumed you were still angry and didn't want us to attend. So I respected that."

"So you're saying after all these years, it was just the mailman's fault?" She couldn't keep the sarcasm out of her tone. It clung to her vocal cords like a poison she couldn't swallow or cough up. "I find that hard to believe."

"I don't know, Caley." Nonie's brow furrowed as if trying to solve a puzzle. "I just can't imagine your father would have received the invitation and not told me."

Oh, Caley could imagine it all right. That was her dad. His way or the highway. Always had been. She hadn't wanted to live by his rules forever, so she would pay the price forever instead.

Even after he was gone.

"I guess we'll never know now." Her voice cracked as tears reached a crescendo in her throat. She coughed before shoving her chair back. "I've got to go, Nonie. I'm sorry, I can't do this. Go ahead and just name the elephant if you want to." Blinded, she stumbled over the chair leg and grabbed for her purse. "Enjoy the cookies. I'll bring Ava by in a few days."

"Caley." Her grandmother's no-nonsense voice froze her feet to the stained floor, but she didn't turn. Couldn't face her. Couldn't uncover anything else that would leave a fresh scar. She was still too wounded by her old ones.

"I'm sorry for my tone, Nonie. I love you." She started to leave, more ashamed than ever, but Nonie spoke again.

"I need you to remember two things."

Her tone, gentler now, coaxed Caley to turn. She reluctantly met her grandmother's stare, one hand braced against the door frame in an effort to hold herself together.

The fire in Nonie's eyes cooled to a steady ember. "I always loved you, my child. And always will."

Caley nodded as the tears crested, slipping down her cheeks. She let them fall on her shirt, unable to let go of the door to wipe them away. "And the second thing?"

"There's more to this situation than you know. When you're ready to find out, you come tell me."

Brady drove slowly down the deserted highway back toward the ranch, thumbs tapping a rhythm on the steering wheel. The noon sun beat hot upon his work truck, nearly blinding him with the glare off the hood. He slid on his sunglasses and adjusted the visor. No wonder all the local news stations had been warning about brush fires. Between the heat and the drought, the soil was cooked dry, not to mention the hay and timber. One well-meaning person with a campfire or burn pile could start an unstoppable chain reaction.

As could one ignorant boy with a cigarette.

Brady shook off the memory before it could set its claws in, and turned at Junction 180. He cast a glance in the rearview mirror at the truck bed loaded with hay. With the drought he hadn't been able to grow enough in his own fields for his cattle this summer—and hay wasn't cheap. Hopefully he could make this load last longer than the previous one, or he'd see red—literally—in his checkbook.

He drove past the county cemetery, about ten miles out from his property, his stomach still tightening with regret every time he glimpsed the familiar oak where Jessica was buried. But today, a flash of red several rows over caught his eye. He slowed down as the crimson blur focused into a human form, crouched on the ground beside a simple marker. A woman.

The wind stirred her hair from her face as one hand reached up to swipe at her eyes.

Caley.

Without thinking, he slammed on the brakes and made a quick turn into the open-gated lot. He parked and slid out of the cab, pocketing his keys as he jogged to her side. "Caley? Are you all right?"

Her blond head lifted, and she looked up in surprise. "Brady! What are you doing here?" She looked around as if searching for a clue to explain why he'd come, black smears lining the corners of her eyes.

"I was driving back from buying hay, and saw you sitting here. You looked— You seemed…" His voice trailed off. She'd seemed upset, but wasn't that normal for someone sitting inside a cemetery? Hardly worthy of a rescue. Yet—whom did she know here? He rolled in his lower lip, unsure how to continue. Then he extended his hand, and helped her stand. "I just wanted to make sure you didn't need a friend."

Friend. The word rolled around his mind and slid off his tongue. He and Caley—friends? In so many ways, it felt like much more.

And in other, more disheartening ways, like so much less.

She stood and slowly withdrew her hand, the surprise in her eyes morphing into something closer to shock—and no wonder, after the heated exchanges they'd had the past few days. He hadn't really acted like a friend, leaving her house so quickly the other night when that blasted pager went off. But then again, friendship clearly hadn't been the first thing on her mind as she tried to tell him how to raise his own daughter, either.

But this wasn't stubborn, fiery Caley insisting she knew best. This was sad, quiet Caley, who looked as though she mourned someone in this graveyard just like he did.

"Did you— Do you…know someone here?" Brady never knew how to regard the dead. In the weeks and months after Jessica died, people kept referring to her in present tense before painfully correcting themselves into the past tense. He hated the effect it left, as if even the person's impact on the earth had vanished along with their body. It wasn't right.

"Know someone here? Unfortunately, not well enough." She gestured to a tombstone with the hand he'd just held, the impression of it still melded into his palm, then shoved her hair back from her face. Her usually neat, shoulder-length cut looked as if it'd been through the wringer, finger-streaked and windblown. And her eyes, red-rimmed and makeup-smeared, were something out of a depressing movie. Yet somehow she'd never looked more beautiful.

She stared at the marker before them. "My dad's grave."

Oh. Brady flinched. Not what he'd expected. "I didn't realize." The words fell flat, and he almost wished he hadn't said anything and just let the chorus of birds chirping overhead fill the silence in the sun-streaked cemetery.

She continued to stare, as if the marker held some sort of control over her. "I never got to say goodbye." She sank back to her knees, not seeming to care the way the dirt stained her jeans.

Brady slowly lowered beside her, crouching on his boots. "What happened?"

"Heart attack." She rubbed at her eyes again, smearing black eye makeup almost to her ear. "I wasn't here." She sniffed.

Her sun-tinted cheeks flushed redder with emotion. She clearly felt guilty about her dad's death, somehow, but he couldn't piece together why. People didn't make other people have heart attacks. Obviously her guilt was misplaced, but without the details, he couldn't help her see that. Nor could he play Twenty Questions to figure it out while she cried over a tombstone.

He cut his eyes to Jessica's marker several yards

away. It'd been too long since he let Ava bring flowers. Did Caley know it was there? Did it even matter? He closed his eyes, briefly reliving that tragic afternoon that changed his life forever. Then, connected by their shared grief, he did the only thing he knew to do.

Sank down in the dirt beside Caley and stained his own jeans.

Chapter Fifteen

"Really? That's excellent news." Caley's heart rate accelerated as she struggled to hear Captain O'Donnell through her lousy cell-phone reception. She pinched one ear shut and strode briskly up Brady's living room stairs, hoping the higher level would solidify the patchy conversation. "I appreciate the update."

"No problem." Captain's deeper voice rumbled through the patchy connection, masked briefly by Ava's moans of homework-related frustration from her room. "Chief is impressed with how many runs you've managed to make during your time back in Broken Bend. He can tell you're a serious candidate for the position."

Caley exhaled a sigh of relief that she quickly turned away from Ava's verbal headache. Thank goodness the chief was seeing her the way she'd hoped. She'd sacrificed sleep, down time to herself and, to be painfully honest, even time with Nonie in order to run whenever that pager buzzed. But once she was hired on the department, her schedule would calm down, and she would have set hours and not have to jump at every alarm.

She'd never thought she, of all people, would be ready for a bit of consistency.

"As long as you keep participating and there aren't any surprises at the annual budget meeting, you should be set." Captain's smile shone through his voice, and not for the first time, Caley wondered what it would have been like to hear that fatherly pride from her dad. Captain barely knew her, but was already impressed—as was Chief Talbot—with Caley's ability and work ethic. Why couldn't her dad have seen the same, have seen her strengths and her destiny to help others, rather than trying to keep her in a box her entire life?

"I won't let you down. Any of you." The promise came from deep inside her heart, and as they disconnected the call, Caley stared at her phone, wishing she could have kept the same commitment to her father. Yesterday's breakdown in the cemetery had been a lot less cathartic than she'd hoped. She'd gone for clarity and closure, and instead, left with more confusion and heartache than ever. Only adding to her confusion was Brady's sudden appearance—the last person she'd expected to see riding up like a knight on a metal, hay-strewn steed.

The memory stirred something warm within her. There she'd been, teary-eyed and drippy, a total mess, crying in public as though her father had died yesterday instead of years ago. But in some ways it felt the same. That's what regret did to a person's soul. Would she ever find a way through it?

Did she deserve to?

The worst part was, she was still angry. Sorry for her part in their fallout, but more than a little upset over his. Neither of them had ever stepped forward to reconcile.

Wasn't that a dad's job, to take the first step? Especially after she'd already made gestures. All he'd had to do was respond. Show up. For the first time in her life, just be there without judgment, without expectation. Just *come*.

Apparently that had still been too much to ask.

But Brady had understood, despite the fact they barely talked. His supportive shoulder and the way he filled the silence with his presence, without finding it necessary to speak, spoke volumes in itself. Despite all their differences, he cared. She didn't know how long they sat kneeling in the dirt, letting the earth seep through their jeans before finally returning to the ranch. She'd gone to her house and he to his, but his departing smile and wave as he rumbled past her driveway had been different, somehow. Deeper. More sincere.

Connected.

A third groan, louder this time, rang from Ava's room. Caley shoved her phone into her pocket and quickly jogged back upstairs to lend homework assistance. Her homework days were far behind her, but even writing lines would beat daydreaming about Brady. Talk about a dead-end road. She knocked on Ava's slightly open door and eased it open, the hinges squeaking.

"Math hates me." Ava stared glumly at the textbook before her on the desk, the pencil in her white-knuckled grip hovering above her notebook full of scratched-out problems. A doodle of a dog that had to be Scooter sat discarded beside the notebook. "And I hate Dad's rule about homework being done first on a Friday night. It's the weekend!"

"Rules are rules, kid. Complaining doesn't change them." Caley actually thought that rule of Brady's wasn't a bad one. It definitely prevented any late-Sunday-night panic over unfinished work. She hip-bumped Ava half out of the desk chair. "Scoot over and let me see." She bent over the book and determined the topic. "Fractions, huh?"

"We're not even allowed to use a calculator." Ava flopped her head down on her crossed arms in true preteen, drama-queen fashion. "And Mandy was supposed to come over after dinner, but now I'll never finish."

"Sure you will. The key is not getting so worked up that you can't even think. Deep breaths." Caley skimmed the problems while Ava inhaled and exhaled, then worked a few on the notepad. She tapped Ava with the pencil when she finished. "It's not that bad. You just have to focus." She pointed to one of the attempts Ava had scratched out. "You almost had it here."

Caley walked a reluctant Ava through several problems before an understanding light began to shine in her eyes. "I think I get it now." She did the next problem on her own, and Caley knew without checking it was correct.

"Good job! See, you just can't give up." She gave Ava a quick hug before slipping out of the chair to give her space to work. "Giving up means you immediately lose."

"That's what usually happens." Ava wrinkled her nose, half turning in her chair. "When I get stuck on a problem, Dad and I start arguing and we give up."

Caley nodded slowly. Understandable, but not a great model for education. However, she sensed this wasn't really about math anymore. Ava was comparing Caley with her dad. And that was what was doing the most damage to Brady. She'd seen it before when Ava mentioned she'd rather Caley help her clean her room than her dad. And every instance that Brady had to turn her down for being busy with ranch work. He *had* to go, yet Caley was still there by default as her nanny.

And, to be honest, she was here because she wanted to be. She hated watching the strain between Ava and her dad, and anything she could do to ease the gap for Ava, she wanted to do it. The whole situation was too painfully familiar. Yet it seemed Brady's heart was softer than her own father's had been. He loved Ava, that much was evident—he just didn't seem to know what to do with her.

But had her involvement in Ava's life pushed Brady further away instead of drawing him closer to his daughter?

She chose her next words carefully. "Ava, different people have different strengths. Your dad might not be as naturally inclined toward math as I am. But there's a lot of things he's good at that I'm not." Like laying down roots. Committing to one place, one community, for a lifetime. She swallowed the examples. Specifics wouldn't help right now—especially with Ava seeming as naturally stir-crazy in her heart as Caley had been at her age. No need to plant ideas in the girl's head that would just make her miserable. Besides, Ava's current issue didn't seem to be her desire to leave or live elsewhere, so much as it seemed she just wanted her dad's undivided attention.

Somehow, Caley would make sure she got it.

"Is that why people get married?" Ava hung one arm over the back of her chair, pencil dangling from her fingers. "To help each other when the other person isn't good at something?"

Caley stumbled back a step before catching herself on the side of Ava's bed. She swallowed her surprise at the sudden change in topic and sank onto the bedspread. "Uh, that's one benefit to marriage, yes."

"You and my dad would make a good team." A slight smile lit Ava's face. "You'd be strong where he was weak."

"And vice versa," Caley automatically corrected. Then sucked in a regretful breath. Her choice of words made it sound as if she was giving her agreement. Hopefully Ava wouldn't notice or think that—

"Yep. And vice versa." Ava's grin morphed into a near beam of light.

Something smelled good. *Really* good. He hoped whatever it was didn't end up on the kitchen floor—or in the trash can.

Brady stomped his boots a few times on the entry mat, then hurried to peek inside the oven. A rush of hot air and the tangy aroma of oregano and cheese blasted his face—followed by a solid *whap* on his shoulder.

He let the door snap shut and turned to see Caley armed with an oven mitt and a feisty smile. "No peeking. This is Ava's surprise."

"Ava cooked?" He moved away from the oven and her weapon of choice, then realized that decision put him perfectly in line with the freshly baked garlic bread cooling on the counter. He broke off the end of the loaf and popped it into his mouth, dodging Caley's second assault with the mitt. The bread practically melted against his tongue, and he resisted the urge to suggest maybe his daughter give Caley cooking lessons. He'd take a steady beating with that mitt in exchange for another bite of bread any day. His stomach growled, and he went to grab a second pinch but Caley moved it out of his way.

"She sure did. And don't go in the dining room. She's creating a special place setting, and apparently it's a surprise, too. She's really getting responsible." Caley started to say more but a knock on the front door interrupted. She held up one finger to indicate for him to wait—and probably to also stay off the bread.

"Ava! Your friend is here." She backed out of the kitchen and hollered toward the formal dining room. Brady swallowed as he eyed the closed doors across the hall. They hadn't used that room since…when? The holidays last year. And even then, it'd felt pointless. Like a charade. Like they were some kind of fancy, proper family gathered around a perfectly stuffed goose, surrounded by mistletoe and holly and spiced gumdrops.

Last Christmas, he and Ava had dined on ham sandwiches, baked beans and a frozen apple pie.

Caley checked the timer on the oven, then shot an apologetic glance his direction. "Ava said you told her it was okay for Mandy to come over after dinner, but after we finished her homework and she cooked, she was so excited she asked if Mandy could eat with us. She asked me to stay, too." She donned a second mitt and removed the bubbling dish from the oven. Brady had half a mind to grab it from her, but decided not making sudden movements was probably safer. For both his sake and that of his dinner. "I hope that was okay. I went outside to ask you but you weren't in the barn."

"Of course." Was he so strict they thought he'd mind if Caley stayed and ate? He didn't even know how to answer that. Then her words finally registered. "You mean Ava did her homework *and* cooked all this?" He waved his hand around the kitchen, noting a full salad in a bowl by the sink, already tossed. He hadn't realized they'd had lettuce in the house. It didn't even look bagged. "What about her math?"

"Math is done, along with spelling words and

notecards for her science project." Caley deposited the saucy, cheesy concoction that resembled some sort of lasagna on top of the stove.

Brady couldn't help but follow her every movement, afraid to fully recognize how natural she looked in his kitchen. How he could watch her bustle around and multitask in his home as if it was her own all day long with zero complaints. His mouth dried, and he was suddenly overcome with the crazy urge to tell her that. "Caley?" Oops. He hadn't meant to say it out loud.

She turned toward him, a smear of sauce dotting the corner of her mouth and her upraised hands still encased in mitts. She looked adorable—cute enough he could almost forget all their differences.

Almost.

He reached forward, the urge still there but now restrained, and swiped the sauce from her face. "I just busted you for taste testing."

Her eyes, wide and luminous with unasked questions, dimmed briefly before igniting with her typical spark. "Guilty. Ava insisted on extra onion powder, and I had to make sure it wasn't a bad idea."

Would she even know if it was? He wanted to tease her about her cooking skills, but he feared the banter would lead to more moments he couldn't resist. In just a few minutes, he'd have more than enough emotion to fight, sitting with

Caley and Ava around their dining room table like a real family.

The doorbell chimed and Caley quickly removed the mitts. "I guess I better get the door after all." She strode past the dining room, calling for Ava a second time just as she rushed out.

"I got it!" Ava sidestepped Caley and shut the dining room door behind her, then practically ran for the entryway. "Hope you enjoy your dinner, Dad." She flashed him a smile, one without lingering traces of their argument yesterday, and Brady smiled in return as he followed her to the front door. His daughter, growing up. Cooking supper. Doing her chores. What was that Caley had said about responsibility? Maybe—

"See you guys tomorrow." Ava shouldered a duffel bag that seemed to appear out of nowhere and wrenched the door open.

A humid breeze wafted through the entryway and Mandy grinned from the front steps. "Hi, Mr. McCollough. Thanks for letting Ava spend the night."

"What? Wait a second." Brady reeled backward, nearly tripping over Caley, who had come up behind him. He caught his balance. Ava spend the night at her house? Mandy was staying with *them*. His head raced. "What about dinner?"

Ava rushed outside as if she hadn't heard, grabbing Mandy's hand and dragging her down the front walk toward her mother's van. Mandy's mom waved from the front window, all smiles. She clearly wasn't surprised. Had he misunderstood? He replayed the conversation he and Ava had that morning before school, when she'd asked to invite a friend over. No, he wasn't mistaken.

So much for responsibility. Ava was already shutting the van door behind her. He lifted one hand in a wave back at Mandy's mom, pressing his lips together into a tight line and debating rushing down the driveway and hauling Ava back inside. The problem wasn't Mandy's house, she'd stayed there a dozen times before. It was the deceit. Ava had lied—or purposefully misled him. Either way, she couldn't get away with it, or this wouldn't be the last time. He took a step toward the van.

A cool hand on his forearm stilled his booted feet. Caley. "Don't embarrass her. It was just a misunderstanding."

"A misunderstanding? I don't think so." Brady shook his arm free of her grip, not in the mood for interference. Especially from someone who had already made things worse between him and his daughter—even if unintentionally.

All the attraction he'd been fighting moments ago in the kitchen melted into a hot wave of frustration. Caley might have been hired to watch his daughter, but he hadn't hired her to drive a wedge further between them. He was sick of being compared to his nanny and coming up short. He clenched his fist at his side, wishing he had a hay bale to sling, and took a deep breath before speaking. "She asked me specifically if Mandy could spend the night here. What's so confusing about that?"

Caley flinched at his hardened tone, and he reeled his temper in, clamping his mouth shut. He wasn't being fair. This wasn't Caley's fault. It was Ava's.

And probably his own.

By then, the van had backed out of the driveway and was halfway down the street. He shut the door harder than he should have, his good mood over Ava's surprise dinner ruined. One good surprise didn't cancel out a bad one. What had she been thinking?

"I don't understand, then." Caley crossed her arms over her sleeveless top, eyes wary as if he were a dog she wasn't sure would bite her or not. "Why would Ava go to so much trouble to cook for you if she wasn't going to be here to see you eat it?"

"I don't know." But he'd definitely be finding out. Soon. Brady headed to the kitchen for the cordless phone, then realized the girls hadn't had time to make it to Mandy's house yet. He'd have to wait.

He slammed the phone back into its base and

ran his hands through his hair. If Ava was this deceitful over a simple slumber party with a friend, what choices would she make once she started driving in a few years? Once she discovered boys? His stomach twisted. He had to nip this in the bud, *now.* Before it barreled out of control like a fire in a basement cellar.

He grabbed his truck keys off the counter. If he couldn't call Ava, then he'd go after her.

"Um, Brady?" Caley's soft voice called from the hallway, timid and unsure. Not at all like herself. "I think you need to see this."

It must be bad if she was holding him back from his mission. He quickly joined her in front of the dining room. Then his jaw slacked open. The formal table was set with the floral-print heirloom china passed down from his mother-in-law, multiple pieces arranged carefully around each place setting. Tall stemware glasses sat at the ready beside a pitcher of iced tea, and a jumble of candles rose above a crowd of carefully arranged dried flowers that served as a centerpiece on the table.

A table set for two.

Chapter Sixteen

The sneaky little matchmaker.

Caley wiped her fingers on the linen napkin in her lap, torn between wanting to smirk at Brady attempting to figure out which fork to use for his lasagna, and cry with frustration over the situation Ava had put herself in—and consequently, Caley, too. Talk about one step forward, three steps back. If only Ava had seen the pride in her dad's face, heard the wonder in his voice when he realized how much she'd accomplished that day. How much the effort had meant to him personally.

Ava had clearly decided her new, bow-and-heart-shaped-arrow mission was more important for the moment than winning over her dad.

A futile mission, at that. She thought Brady had been about to—well, she didn't know what, but he'd had intentions in his eyes in the kitchen that went beyond busting her for sneaking a taste of the lasagna before dinnertime. Then with the first sign of Ava's deceit, he'd reverted back into overprotective dad on the warpath. The look on his face when she'd stopped him from storming after Ava had resembled nothing short of accusation. As though this whole stunt was *her* fault.

Men.

Caley stole a glance at Brady, who had shoveled half his salad into his mouth before bothering to speak to her. Apparently she was now paying some sort of silent price for convincing him to eat before making any rash decisions about Ava. He'd broken the awkward quiet only once, when he'd gruffly asked her to pass the garlic bread. She'd been tempted to lob it at his head.

She'd beat him at his own game, except she was pretty sure he could stay silent for a lot longer than she could.

With a sigh, she turned her attention back to her dinner, trying to convince herself it didn't matter what Brady thought—or what he did. Because every time she felt a connection between them, a breakthrough, something like this happened that morphed him straight back into a present-day, cowboy-hat-donning version of her dad.

No, thanks.

She speared a tomato with her salad fork, impressed Ava had known the difference in size. She must have been paying attention during her home-economics class at school. Caley shook her head in wonder at the elaborate table setting. She'd even found crystal napkin rings that Caley felt fairly certain had never been used.

Or at least, had not been used since Mrs. McCollough died.

Her frustration at Brady's dramatic reaction to Ava's shenanigans sobered. Was that part of the explanation for the shadows in his expression? The dark bags under his eyes? Maybe sitting here, surrounded by floral-print reminders of the past, just made him miss his wife.

Something stark and cold—something a lot like jealousy—pressed a fist into Caley's stomach. She set her napkin on the table, through eating despite the half stick of bread still on her plate. Scooter would eat it. She'd lost her appetite, and refused to try to acknowledge why. Not tonight. Not with grumpy ol' Papa Bear still gobbling his porridge across the table.

Not with the touch of his finger against her mouth still burning her lips.

Brady's dark eyebrows rose as Caley pushed back from the table and began to clear her plates. "You're done?"

So he could speak. And those simple words pressed a red warning button deep inside her system. "Oh, I'm done all right." Done with his mood

swings, done with the unwanted chemistry—
apparently unwanted both ways—and done with
his ignorance of his daughter's needs. The dishes
clanked as she stacked the salad bowl on top of
the dinner plate, punctuating her anger. "Do you
even have any idea why Ava did this?" She gestured around the dining room, suddenly, irratio-
nally hating the fact that Brady hadn't bothered
to light the candles.

Brady stopped midchew, then swallowed and
wiped his mouth with his napkin. The crisp linen
looked totally out of place in his callused hands,
somehow making Ava's gesture seem all the
sweeter. Her method of delivery might have been
wrong, but the heart behind the entire plan had
been intentional. Considerate, in its own way. Yet
Brady only saw the broken rules.

He picked up his tea glass, the amber liquid already appearing watered down. "I think it's clear.
She's matchmaking."

He didn't meet her eyes when he said the words,
and she didn't blame him. It was awkward—but
only because they both refused to name the un-
dercurrent between them.

One problem at a time. Caley planted her hands
on her hips, her level of indignation on Ava's be-
half—and if she was honest, her own—rising to

dangerous heights. "She wasn't thinking about misleading you. She was concocting a surprise."

"It wasn't just misleading me. It was a bald lie." His cheeks flushed red and he stood, Ava's carefully decorated table separating them.

"She had tonight all planned, Brady. She's been trying to think of ways to impress you and earn your trust. Earn more responsibility." Caley grabbed the stack of dishes and left the room with them, giving Brady no choice but to follow or end the conversation. Either way worked for her. She didn't want to fight, but couldn't let him believe the worst about his daughter just because of surface appearances.

Just like that night her and her dad's relationship was ruined for good—the night she told him she had signed up for the Peace Corps and wouldn't be going to the local community college. While she knew he'd be caught off guard, she hadn't expected the blowup that had ensued. Or Nonie's lack of interference. If Nonie had spoken up, defended her, would her dad have changed his mind? Would the entire past decade of her life have been written differently?

She couldn't sit by and let Ava suffer in silence. The girl definitely needed to be reprimanded for the way she carried out her plan, but more than that, Brady needed to see the truth behind her motives.

"Earn responsibility?" Brady's voice called from the dining room, where the clanking of plates indicated he was clearing his spot, as well. "I don't see how pulling a sudden move like this one was going to win her that particular prize."

She raised her voice to be heard in the next room. "You're right. You don't see anything at all." Then she whirled around to get the next batch of dishes from the dining room, but ran into Brady's hard chest instead. She put her hands up to cushion the impact, but his free hand immediately went to the counter next to her, blocking her escape.

"What don't I see?" His breath, warm and spicy, tingled the fine hairs at the curve of her neck.

She fought back a shiver, determined not to reveal his effect on her. "You don't see what's right in front you." She refused to look up and make eye contact at such close proximity, focusing instead on the muscular curve of his shoulders beneath the smooth lines of his shirt. Maybe that wasn't such a good idea, either, because she was starting to forget why she was so mad.

"I see plenty."

She risked a glance, and his hair, free of its typical hat confinement, fell across his forehead and flirted with his strikingly blue eyes. Big mistake. "Like what?" She looked away before daring to glance back, curiosity—and despite knowing better, a rogue flash of hope—getting the best of her control.

"I see you're a woman who knows what she wants." He brushed a tendril of hair from her forehead before anchoring his arm back to the counter beside her. "A woman who cares deeply about others. Maybe too much at times."

Her breath caught in her throat at the smirk turning up the corners of his mouth.

"I see you're a woman who can drive me up the wall crazy one minute…" His hand found hers on the countertop, his work-roughened fingers grazing her own. "And the next…" He leaned in closer, and her resolve weakened. Was he going to kiss her? Did she want him to? Yes. No. A thousand contradictions ran through her mind in an exhausting race, finally ending with one truth.

She refused to start something neither of them could finish.

"I was talking about Ava." She pressed against his shoulders, and he hesitated only a moment before stepping out of her way. She avoided his gaze, not wanting to see the disappointment in his eyes—or worse, see that there wasn't any.

They cleared the rest of the table in silence, and Caley began to load the dishwasher before realizing those china plates should be hand washed. With a sigh, she turned on the hot water and began filling the sink.

Brady turned from putting the salad bowl back in the refrigerator. "I'll get those later."

"In a hurry to get rid of me?" The words slipped out, tasting as bitter as they sounded. She clenched her lips. What was she doing?

His eyes darkened as he studied her. "Sometimes you seem in a big hurry to leave."

She pressed her fingers against her temples, remaining silent while Brady reached around her and shut off the water.

"Come sit with me." He took her hand and led her to the front door. She was too drained to argue.

They settled on opposite ends of the dusty porch swing, and Brady pushed them off with his feet. Around them, late-evening crickets chirped from the trees. An autumn breeze rustled her hair, and she turned her face into it, allowing the caress to cool her flushed cheeks and release the tension gnawing at her shoulders.

Brady's quiet voice broke through the squeaking of the swing's rusty chains. "What do you need to say about Ava? It's obviously important to you."

Ava. Was that why she felt a lead weight in her chest? Partially. But not completely. She took a deep breath, trying to dislodge the stone of regret, hating how distant she felt from Brady all of a sudden. From God. From her entire life.

But it was her fault. She'd pulled away from Brady—and from God. Turned them both down in various ways. She didn't have enough of herself anymore to give. But even though it was for their own good, it hurt. Feeling so disconnected was beginning to wax old.

She tensed, struggling to keep her focus. She was here for Ava, on all counts. God approved of that. And whether Brady approved or not, she couldn't help it. She had to intervene. "Ava messed up tonight, Brady. We both know that. But you don't see what she sacrificed."

"What do you mean?" He shifted slightly toward her, the evening shadows casting hard planes across his profile.

"The original plan was to surprise you. She's desperate to show you how responsible she can be. Desperate to show you she can pull her weight around here and be a real help to you." Caley lowered her voice despite their being the only two outside. "She just wants you to notice her."

"So how did she go from that plan to the stunt she pulled tonight?" Brady pushed with his feet, rocking the swing harder as if emphasizing his lingering frustration.

"Because there was something she suddenly wanted more."

He snorted. "What in the world would that be?"

Caley planted her feet on the ground to stop the swing, reaching up and grabbing the chain as she met Brady's gaze with her own. "Us."

* * *

Brady's head spun, and not from the sudden jolt of Caley stopping the swing. He knew Ava had been playing matchmaker—that was clear, with the not-so-subtle table for two and some of the teasing comments he'd heard between Ava and Max. But that was banter. This was legit. Ava wanted Caley to be a part of their family badly enough that she'd risk his and her relationship even further?

He didn't know how he felt about that. He'd obviously had his own feelings for Caley, and to be honest he still struggled with them. It was sort of nice to know Ava was on the same page he'd been on.

Been. Past tense.

Right. Who was he kidding? He still felt the same way for Caley, but it didn't matter. She wasn't what he needed in a wife, if he even needed one at all. And he would only hold her back. That much was clear.

Hopelessness stirred inside him—along with a hearty dose of jealousy. Caley thought she was helping, but how could she, when Ava preferred Caley to him in every situation? Sure, she saw Caley more often, but that wasn't in his control. He was a rancher. He had to provide for his family, not let Ava's inheritance slip down the drain because he was inside playing paper dolls. And he couldn't risk Ava tagging along after him.

If he hadn't kept Jessica safe, how could he keep Ava safe? Losing his wife had cracked his heart open once. He couldn't risk losing his daughter, too, or he'd shatter completely.

"I thought her plan was more obvious than that." Caley's soft voice broke through the white noise in his head, reeling him back in. "I didn't mean to completely shock you."

"You didn't. I mean, well, you did." Brady bent forward on the still swing, bracing his forearms against his thighs. "I knew she had entertained thoughts of you and me, but not to that extent." Not to the extent of Ava practically shoving them toward a justice of the peace. Did she just want Caley around 24/7? Was he even involved in the equation at all?

"She's a good kid." Caley shifted beside him, turning sideways and pulling her jeans-clad legs up on the swing underneath her. A brief shimmer of moonlight shone above the tree line before disappearing behind a bank of gray clouds. "Do you want my advice?"

"Would it even matter if I said no?" He was kidding. Sort of.

Caley smirked, then her eyes grew serious. "Don't be too hard on her for this one. Her actions weren't thought out very well, but…it's important to me that you see her heart here."

"Are you suggesting that I don't punish her?" That was out of the question. If he didn't pony up some consequences, what would Ava try to get away with next?

"I didn't say that. Just talk to her first. Make sure the punishment fits the crime. She's not a perpetually sneaky or misbehaving child, is she?" Caley raised her eyebrows, tilting her head toward Brady with expectation, as if she already knew the answer.

And she did, because he did, too. "No. She's not." Caley was right. He needed to think this one through before he set them even further back. But that didn't explain Caley's cryptic attitude about the whole thing. "Why is this so important to you? I mean, I know you care about Ava, but you've only known her a few weeks." Known him, too, though in many ways it felt like a lot longer. He shifted on the swing to face her, pulling one knee up and pushing them off with his other foot.

She rubbed her hands up her bare arms, and he wished he had a jacket to give her. "It's personal."

"I'm a person." He nudged her booted foot with his, and a smile crept up the corners of her mouth.

"I was actually thinking of you more like a grizzly bear a little while ago."

"Touché." He'd been closer to growling than

he'd liked, especially at Caley. He sobered. "I'm sorry for how I acted at dinner." He averted his gaze to the moon, but it had yet to reappear behind the cloud cover. "I tend to overreact."

"Never would have guessed." The teasing light in her eyes flickered, then slowly faded as she stared across the dark porch. "It's important to me because in a lot of ways, I'm Ava."

He didn't get it, but he let her take her time explaining, giving her his full attention. He had a feeling he didn't need to miss this.

"I grew up here in Broken Bend." Her words, so soft they were almost carried away by the breeze, floated between them.

"Broken Bend doesn't have the best memories for me. My mom left us for another man when I was little." She tilted her chin toward him. "And like a certain fifth grader you know, I had an overprotective dad myself."

Brady started to argue, then clamped his jaw shut. He *was* overprotective. But no one else had a story like his. This, however, was Caley's turn to share.

He still didn't know if he'd take a turn or not.

He cleared his throat. "Go on."

She wrapped her arms around her drawn knees. "Growing up, Dad and I fought all the time. I was the square peg, and he was the round hole. We just didn't fit. Everything I wanted to do he thought was dangerous, and everything he wanted just felt like a trap. I wanted to get out of Broken Bend since I was in junior high."

"Why was that?" Brady loved everything about Broken Bend, from the land his family had sweated and bled over for generations, to the small-time feel of the town, where everyone knew everyone. Sure, the gossip had its disadvantages, as did the unsolicited advice that came from everyone acting like everyone else's mama. But Broken Bend was home. Always would be.

"Nonie said I was born a gypsy." She shook her head, a wry grin briefly lifting her cheeks. "I just wanted more. Wanted to travel, see the rest of the country. Do something that mattered. So I joined the Peace Corps and immediately got a taste of World War Three, but not overseas. Here on the home front."

"Because your dad wanted to keep you nearby." He nodded in understanding. Who could blame Mr. Foster? Brady was starting to want Caley nearby all the time, too, but look where that notion had gotten him. Completely lost, arguing over fancy dishes and having heart-to-heart talks on the porch swing.

As though they were already married.

He shook off the idea. "There are worse things than a caring father, you know." He drew in a tight breath, wishing Caley could see his point of view. He didn't know why Mr. Foster had been the way he was, but Brady knew from experience that being overprotective usually came with a reason. A good one.

Caley's voice turned hard. "Oh, I know. He went from controlling every move I made to disowning me." Her voice caught. "And then he was gone."

Brady's heart wrenched, just like it had when watching her in the cemetery. He didn't know what to say, so he dropped his leg off the swing and scooted over until he could wrap his arm around her. She stiffened, then relaxed against his embrace.

He tilted his head down, wishing he had the right to brush a kiss against her forehead, and instead inhaled the fresh scent of her hair. "I'm sorry." He whispered against her head, not even sure if she'd heard him.

She just snuggled closer, and he held her silently. Times like these he wished he and God were still on speaking terms so he could pray. Back in the days when he believed God actually cared for him and his family, actually had a plan for their lives. But the God he knew in childhood hadn't shown up after Jessica's accident. Either He wasn't in control after all, or He didn't care enough to intervene in tragedy.

It was better to just handle things himself. At least then if he messed up, it was his own fault.

Just like the accident. No more disappointment or shot-down hopes. He was on his own. That's why he couldn't risk anything happening to Ava. He had to take every precaution possible—even if it put them at odds.

Caley finally lifted her head, but didn't pull completely away. "I never got over it, how estranged we were for so long. And me and Nonie, too, by default. She helped raise me, but she was loyal to her son." She took a shuddering breath before wiping her eyes with the back of her hand. "I just wanted one more chance with him, to see if as adults we could agree to disagree. But he didn't even come to my college graduation. After that, I knew it was over. I made my own path in life, finally got to live the way I wanted to, accomplishing things most parents would be impressed over. Becoming a firefighter, getting my EMT. Skydiving. Mountain climbing. Steer roping. I just wanted to live out loud, you know?" She lifted one shoulder in a weary shrug. "But he never understood. He just wanted me to stay right here in Broken Bend, go to college, get a local job." She sighed. "Basically, waste my gifts."

Brady winced. He and Mr. Foster would have unfortunately hit it off well. He wanted the same for Caley—wanted her to give up her thrill-seeking life and stay in Broken Bend permanently. Be there for him and for Ava.

But that wasn't who she was.

The realization made him hurt to his core. Not that it was a surprise, but to hear firsthand how deep-rooted that roaming lifestyle was in her heart…it erased any remnant of hope he'd clung to about things changing in the future.

"I just don't want to see you and Ava make the same mistakes." A stray tear slipped down Caley's cheek, and he gently brushed his finger across her face to catch it. She closed her eyes, leaning slightly into his touch. "Trust me. Some mistakes can be permanent."

No kidding. He'd learned that the hard way with Jessica. For the first time since Caley's arrival next door, he finally understood why she cared so much about his relationship with Ava. She'd been there.

The question was, what was he doing to do about it?

A tree frog croaked nearby, and Brady remembered all those nights camping out as a kid that nature's lullaby would sing him to sleep. For a wild moment, he wondered what would happen if he shared that with Ava. What would it be like to have that connection with her that he'd had with his dad? Despite his older age, Brady's father would sleep in a tent with him in the back pasture in the heat of summer, while his mom sneaked them s'mores and Dr. Pepper. They'd make different animal calls and shadow puppets with their hands, and tell scary stories until Brady insisted on going back to the safety of a night-light and four walls.

Caley's story was testament enough to how holding on too tightly could push a loved one away. If Mr. Foster had given Caley a little bit of lead rope, would she have stuck around? There was no way to know.

But there *was* time to test the theory with Ava.

He stood abruptly as an idea flashed through his mind, reaching down to tug on Caley's hand. "Come on. I want to show you something."

She willingly followed him, which just made him ache all the more.

Chapter Seventeen

Caley followed Brady down the porch steps and across the backyard to the barn, where the moon reflected off the roof's white trim and sparkled like snow. He still had a hold on her hand, and her feet struggled to keep up with his longer strides. What was he doing? How did they go from tear wiping and heart pouring to almost jogging toward the barn? She'd worked with men her entire adult life, but still couldn't figure out their mental connections.

She quickened her pace, then nearly ran into the back of him as he stopped short in front of the barn.

"I have a surprise." He grinned down at her, the mischievous spark in his eyes more reminiscent of a teenage boy on the loose than a stoic grown man with scars. She looked away before that spark could ignite in her stomach, startling when he suddenly cranked open the door with a loud squeak. Low-bulb security lights flashed on in the corners, just dim enough to see by. He grabbed a flashlight that sat on a feed barrel by the door, then motioned for her to follow.

Hard to say no, since he still held her hand. Not that she would have, anyway. After their talk on the porch, an uncharacteristic vulnerability swelled in her heart. She loved the comfort the rough texture of his palm against hers brought, especially after dredging up all her own wounds. Innocent as the physical contact was—and temporary as it was—it was a nice punctuation to their evening.

Tomorrow would bring reality back quickly enough.

The pungent scent of hay assaulted her nose as they strolled by sleepy horses, some wheezing in their sleep, others waking to pop curious heads over stall doors. Brady led her to the back corner stall, double in size compared to the rest, and glanced over the tall rail before handing her the flashlight. "What do you think?"

She warily took the light and let go of his hand, tiptoeing to the stall door and stretching to see over the top. Then she gasped, quickly moving the light to shine it away from the animals' eyes. "The mare had her foal."

"Yesterday. It's a filly." Brady's voice held as

much pride as if he'd orchestrated the entire event himself. "The newest member of the Double C ranch."

"She's so cute." Caley shone the light where she could see into the shadows but not alarm the foal. The baby's matted hair puffed in little waves against her slender frame, but despite her small stature, she braced on all four legs and nuzzled for milk. "What will you name her?"

Brady hesitated, hooking his thumb in his front pocket. "I was thinking about letting Ava decide."

Caley's gaze shot to his and held, her breath catching with hope. If he was going to let Ava name the foal, then did that mean...

"I think maybe you're right. About Ava needing more responsibility." He released a sigh that sounded as if it resonated from the deepest part of his soul. "What you said made a lot of sense. I still want her to be safe, but maybe if she learns how to handle a horse at this size, she could work her way up as she grows up, too."

The hesitancy in his voice cried out for confirmation of his decision, though she knew he'd never ask outright. She set the flashlight on the ground and reached for his hand again, throat thick with emotion. This was a milestone, however small. He'd come a long way. "I think she's going to do great." She swallowed as he moved closer. "And so will you."

"I don't know why it's so important to have your faith in me, Caley, but it is." He stood directly in front of her, reaching up with his free hand to tuck her hair behind her ear. "I downright need it."

She closed her eyes as his thumb grazed her cheek, and his forefinger brushed across her lips, the touch callused but gentle. "You're a good father, Brady. You need more faith in yourself."

"I lost it." His hand cupped the back of her neck, urging her forward. "But you give me hope."

This time, she didn't resist, but willingly stepped into his embrace. Their lips met, hesitantly, then with more confidence as the kiss built, a growing tidal wave of attraction, vulnerability and need. Caley stretched onto her toes, sliding her arms around his neck and clutching the collar of his shirt as his hands buried in her hair, briefly acknowledging that in all her years of wandering, she'd never felt more at home than in Brady's arms.

Behind them, the mare nickered, and they quickly broke apart. Caley reached up to touch her lips, sure they were as red as Brady's, as he awkwardly stepped back and ran a hand through his hair. He gave her a sheepish grin. "I guess maybe we should start sitting on opposite ends of that swing."

She laughed, startling the mare and foal, and quickly covered her mouth with her hand. Shoving aside all her inner reservations, she let her feelings shine in her eyes as she met his gaze. "I sort of liked sharing the middle."

He reached out and looped one arm around her waist, bringing her back close. This time a tender connection still held them both in place. He locked her in his grip, bending down to rest his forehead against hers. "I'm not used to sharing, Caley. I might not be good at it anymore."

"Do you miss her?" She had to know, despite the terrible timing of the question.

His arm stiffened around her waist, and he shook his head. "I regret what happened. I hate that Ava doesn't have a mom anymore. But no, *I* don't miss her. Not the way you're meaning." He hesitated, eyes darkening with emotion she couldn't determine. "Saying that out loud sounds so terrible. But we were so different. Everyone was shocked when we got married."

"What happened, Brady?" She reached around her back to find his hand, clinging to his fingers. "It seems the whole town knows but me, yet no one will say." Would he finally confide in her? Trust her with the broken pieces of his heart? She'd shown him the cracked edges of her own. Would he meet her halfway?

Would it even matter if he did?

She started to ease away as his hesitancy expounded, the words *never mind* ripe on her tongue.

If he didn't want to share, she shouldn't push him—even if that truth did rip her apart.

"I killed her."

All her doubts fell away at his painful admission. "Brady." She pressed her hand against his chest, his heartbeat erratic under her palm. "No." She didn't believe him, not even a little.

"Not directly." He stepped away from her touch, turning sideways and bracing his arms against the stall wall. "But I'm still responsible."

She felt his absence like the prick of a knife but fought the urge to chase him. "How?"

He let out a sharp huff of air. "We were fighting all the time. Just too different. She was happiest in a department store, trying on some fancy shoe, while I, well…" He looked up briefly at the ceiling. "You know me."

She did. And unfortunately kept growing to like what she saw more and more. "What happened?"

"We'd seen a counselor a few times, who kept telling us we had to get interested in the same things. Meet in the middle, if we wanted our marriage to have a chance—and we both did, for Ava's sake." Brady shook his head. "So one day Jessica came out of the house while I was working and saddled up this stallion I'd just bought. He was about as green broke as a garden gnome. But she wanted to impress me. She'd never ridden a day in her life. But I thought she knew how dangerous it was."

His voice caught and Caley couldn't help herself. She touched his shoulder, grateful he didn't shrug away. "And?"

"He threw her. I saw her up there and was so surprised, I didn't say anything at first. I should have demanded she get down. But truth to be told, I was impressed. That she'd make such an effort..." His voice trailed off. "I should have ordered her off immediately. Should have been there sooner. Been closer. When he reared up, she fell."

She could picture it, and the visual made her stomach hurt. "That's not your fault, Brady."

He beat the wooden stall with his fist, and Caley flinched, jerking away. "I should have been there, Caley. I should have caught her." He clutched the top of the stall door so hard his knuckles turned white. "I should have made the first gesture, not her."

"How could you have known?"

"I put work first, even back then. I know it's my fault." He shrugged, the gesture so helpless it tore at Caley's heart. "I wasn't there."

"So that's why you're afraid to let Ava near the animals." The truth dawned, opening her eyes with painful revelation. Why hadn't he said so sooner? It all made sense now. Did Ava even know what happened?

As if reading her mind, Brady glanced at the foal, his expression softening. "Ava doesn't know the gory details. At the time, I didn't want her afraid of everything." He snorted. "Ironic, isn't it?"

"You did what you thought best. But, Brady, none of this is your fault." She could tell he didn't believe her, and she figured she wasn't the first one to try to convince him of the truth.

"I've been there, Caley. I've seen what a little bit of carelessness can do, and I can't risk letting my daughter be in harm's way. What if I can't catch her, either?" His voice cracked, and he cleared his throat. "Maybe I come down too hard on her, but she's alive. She's safe. I've seen what making the wrong choices can do, how choosing the wrong friends can lead you down a path you never intended…."

"Ava is a good kid, Brady," she broke in. "If you're determined to blame yourself for all the bad stuff these past few years, you have to claim the good things, too. She has good friends because you taught her to choose wisely."

He shot her a sideways look. "Good friends who help her trick me into sleepovers."

"You don't know if Mandy knew all the details or not."

"I thought I had good friends when I was Ava's age." Brady picked up the flashlight Caley had set on the barn floor and tapped it absently against his palm. "Turns out they were experimenting with drugs and smoking. One stupid prank and a careless cigarette later, I was trapped in a burning basement."

Surprise held her tongue hostage, as more visuals she couldn't stand to imagine pummeled her brain. He must have been so terrified. No wonder he was so careful with Ava. He had myriad reasons to be paranoid. She finally found her voice. "I'm so sorry."

"Even now, there's pieces of that nightmare I can't remember. Can't place it. It consumes me more than it should. Caley…" His voice trailed as his tone shifted. "I don't like fire."

The subtle warning note in his voice said more than he'd revealed in the past fifteen minutes. The rock of reality that she'd temporarily shifted during their kiss settled back into her stomach with a thump. He hated fire, and she was a firefighter. He was overprotective and cautious in all things, and she wasn't afraid of taking risks for the greater good.

He was the very roots of Broken Bend—and she was a gypsy.

Saturday morning, Brady's joy in presenting Ava with the foal was tempered only by the memories of what had transpired between him and Caley. Standing in the barn, in that same spot, made him wish he could change. Wish he could erase the bad memories that too often held him hostage. Wish he could be the man he wanted to be, a man unscarred by life.

Ava's beaming smile, however, mended the surface level of the wounds.

"Are you serious, Dad?" She stared at the foal in the stall, then looked back at him, eyes half wary, half delighted. As if she couldn't believe it, which made sense, since he still couldn't believe his decision, either.

Brady nodded, despite his inner reservations. "She's yours. But that means you're responsible for her now. Cleaning her stall and brushing her down." His voice warbled and he coughed to hide it. "I expect to see you out here in the barn with me often."

Scrawny arms gripped him in a hug so tight, it cut off his breath. "Thank you, Daddy."

Daddy. The emotion building behind his eyes didn't stand a chance, and he swiped his lids with his shirt cuff before easing back to speak. "Remember our talk we had earlier, okay?" He tilted her chin up with his finger, still amazed at how grown she looked. "No more secrets or matchmaking or deceit. You leave adult things to the adults. And you never trick me into changing plans with your friends again."

"Yes, sir." Ava grinned at her new pet, who eyed her as curiously as Ava eyed it.

He smiled, wishing Caley could have been here to see this, but she'd insisted last night that it be a private moment between the two of them. As usual, she'd been right. It'd been for the best.

But he still missed her, especially after the way their conversation had ended last night in the barn. After his admission about his past, they'd just stared at each other, each seeing the impasse between them but unwilling to name it further. Then she'd held her breath, rolling in that irresistible bottom lip of hers in concern. "Are you going to change your mind about the foal?"

He'd assured Caley he wouldn't, though his instincts screamed at him to lock Ava in a stone tower. Only he'd remember to cut her hair every so often so a rogue prince wouldn't get any smart ideas.

He'd walked Caley home after that, their hands occasionally brushing in the darkness, but he'd made no move to hold it like he had before. Why complicate things further? He'd screwed up enough, kissing her like that and leading them both to think a relationship between them had a fighting chance.

Yet at the same time, he didn't regret it. Having just that brief taste of Caley's charm and fire and goodness had been worth the heartache that came after, when reality sank its unforgiving claws right back in.

"Can I brush her now?" Ava hopped on the balls of her feet, and he quickly rested his hand on her shoulder to settle her down.

"Yes. But remember, no sudden movements by the horses. You have to be calm so they stay calm." He wasn't sure who would be keeping him calm during this transition, however. He took a long breath. It was taking care of a foal. Not bull riding or barrel racing or anything high-speed or adrenaline-laced. He could do this, one step at a time.

For Ava.

Max suddenly rounded the corner of the barn, and before he could even say *good morning,* Ava tackled him with her good news and a hug. "Uncle Max! I got a horse! A baby." She cleared her throat, lifting her chin. "I mean, a *filly.*"

"Wow." Max peered over her head at Brady, unasked questions in his eyes. "That's definitely a surprise, squirt."

"Go grab a grooming brush for your filly, Ava. And start thinking about names." Brady ruffled her ponytail as she passed, eliciting the typical female protest.

Max waited until Ava was out of sight before he leaned in close to Brady. "Is this for real?"

"Let's just say I had a bit of revelation last night."

"From a certain cute blonde?" Max wiggled his eyebrows.

"No more matchmaking, bro. I can't take it." He pushed up the sleeves of his shirt, suddenly warm inside the barn. "But yes, Caley helped me see some things I needed to change. For Ava."

"What about for yourself?" Max plucked a long strand of hay from the bale nestled in the filly and mare's trough, and began winding it around his finger. "Did she help you figure that out, too?"

"Cut it out." Brady grabbed a straw for himself and settled the end between his teeth.

"I'm serious, man. You and Caley have a connection. You shouldn't throw that away."

"You don't understand."

"Enlighten me." Max turned and crossed his arms, daring Brady with his stance to answer.

Brady pulled the straw from his mouth and crossed his own arms in mirror image. "You remember how different Jessica and I were?"

Max nodded.

"Caley and I make those differences seem downright petty. She's all into living loud, taking risks. Being that way is so important to her that it estranged her and her dad." He plucked at the straw. "I sort of doubt I'm enough to make her change her mind if that wasn't."

"People change, Brady. Give her a chance."

"To be honest, I don't want to." He shook his

head. "Not like that. It's who she is, man. Jessica and I married, each thinking we'd change the other, and were miserable our entire marriage. It just doesn't work that way, no matter how deep the attraction. Or how deep the…" He almost said *love,* but bit it back.

Max heard it anyway. "If you love her, you can't just let her go."

"I know." Brady pulled the straw into two pieces, then slowly let them drop to the ground by his boots. "That's why I'm not going to trap her in the first place."

Chapter Eighteen

Despite her love of adventure and years of protesting her father's regulations, Caley had always been a rule follower. Part of the consequences of living under constant rank at the fire station. But today, she had no qualms about sneaking Scooter into the nursing home for a visit with Nonie.

She adjusted her wiggling, blanket-wrapped parcel, casually nodded her head at a passing nurse, and ducked into Nonie's room.

Empty.

Caley's eyes took in the made bed, the dark TV and the streaks of sunshine pouring through the blinds, and nearly dropped Scooter in surprise. A burst of panic marred her senses, then dismay began a slow seep into her heart. Surely if something had happened, they'd have told her. A phone call, at the least. Right?

"You won't find Ms. Irene in here, honey." The

nurse Caley had passed moments ago popped her head in the doorway, her curly dark hair secured in a tight ponytail.

So…where? Or was that some kind of code for heaven? Her throat dried and she shifted Scooter in her arms, who'd remained uncharacteristically still. Maybe he sensed Caley's distress. She searched the nurse's face for any hint of her worst fear, wishing she could coax her suddenly thick tongue into asking the burning questions.

A cool hand on her arm jerked Caley back to her senses. "Now don't go getting all worked up, honey." The nurse squeezed her forearm with sympathy. "I just meant she's outside in the garden. Asked for some sunshine today."

The garden. Outside. Not in heaven. The words slowly began to make sense, and Caley exhaled a breath she didn't realize she'd been holding. "Okay. The garden. Thank you."

"Out the back doors and to the right." The nurse started to leave, then leaned in toward Caley with a secretive grin, her teeth white against her cocoa-colored skin. "And outside, no one will tell you to put that dog away." She gestured to the blanket in Caley's arms.

A steadfast blush crept up her neck. "Right. Thank you." She wouldn't even pretend to deny it, not with Scooter's black snout now sticking out of the blanket. He whined as if offended she didn't offer any defense, and she shushed him as she hurried outside.

Nonie sat in a rocking chair in a small courtyard, her face tilted toward the sun as her house-shoe-clad feet gently coaxed the chair into rhythm. A thin blanket draped over the shoulders of her housedress, and despite her pale, thin skin, she looked the happiest and most relaxed Caley had seen her since returning to Broken Bend.

"Hi, Nonie." Caley eased into the vacant chair beside her, grateful they had this area of the courtyard to themselves. Across the walking path, an elderly couple held hands as they sat on a stone bench, tossing bread crumbs to an eager squirrel. Nearby, a small fountain trickled water into a shallow pool surrounded by carefully tended flowers.

Nonie opened her eyes and smiled at Caley. "I wondered when you'd show up. Who's that?" She pointed to Scooter, who Caley unwrapped and set on the ground.

She tossed the now hairy blanket on the concrete stepping stones by her feet as Scooter sniffed the wind in the direction of the squirrel. "This is Scooter. I've had him a few years now. I rescued him from a warehouse fire."

Nonie leaned forward in her chair and let Scooter sniff her hand before he lost interest and dismissed her with a quick swipe of his tongue. "He's cute. Ava must love him."

"She does. She's constantly drawing pictures of him or sneaking him treats." Scooter had gained a few pounds since Caley began her job as Ava's nanny, but he didn't seem to mind in the least.

"Ava's a good girl. You bring her next time, you hear?" Nonie folded her hands across the stomach of her housedress and began rocking again. The wind picked up and stirred her unruly tufts of hair. Despite the disobedient strands, her lipstick remained fixed in place.

The sight brought comfort. Caley smiled. "I will. She's with her dad right now, getting a pretty special surprise." She couldn't wait to hear the details about the filly after she got back home.

No. Back to the *ranch*.

Her stomach twisted. Had that kiss with Brady shaken her so badly she'd begun thinking of the ranch as home? She hadn't even thought that way about her rental property. Or anywhere in Broken Bend, for that matter.

Just with Brady.

"Seems like her dad is a pretty special guy, too." Nonie's warm voice cut through the memories of that sizzling kiss, and Caley flushed for the second time since arriving at the nursing home.

"They both are."

"But?"

But. There was always a *but*, wasn't there? Caley took a deep breath, watching as Scooter settled on top of her shoes and began gnawing on a stick. "*But* we're so different, Nonie. It's not even apples to oranges. It's like…apples to pineapple. Or kiwi."

"Sounds like a pretty good fruit salad."

She grinned despite the seriousness of the conversation. "If my life was a buffet, there'd be no problem." Then her smile faded. "I really like him, Nonie." *Like* didn't even begin to cut it. But she refused to tread even further down that dead end, even to herself. "It just won't work. We both know it. He's got baggage that makes mine look like a one-night stay at a budget hotel."

Nonie continued to rock, her gaze riveted on the water fountain before them. "Have you made him my cookies yet?"

"I tried, remember? Epic failure." Caley groaned. "I guess that recipe will die with you." She bit her lip, not having intended to mention dying, but Nonie didn't seem to notice her slip.

"Sounds to me like you have all the ingredients you need. Just got to figure out how to mix them together properly."

They weren't talking about cookies anymore. She shifted her feet, earning a protest from Scooter, who crept away and lay on top of Nonie's slippers instead. "I'm not a good chef. Trust me." *In the kitchen or in the love department.*

"Quit stirring and start blending."

Blended cookies? She frowned. "Nonie, you've lost me."

"Figuratively, dear. Don't you dare go back to that ranch and put my cookie mix into a blender." Nonie chuckled. "You've got to blend all these elements of your life, Caley. Quit compartmentalizing. And let God have the speed control on that blender."

Control. Not something she was very good at giving up. And to God? What if He didn't take any better care of her than her father had? What if He decided to leave her like her mother had?

Wasn't it better to reject first?

But the memories of her childhood lessons at church refused to let go. She'd given God her heart at a young age, but reality and the pressures of life had muddied the once crystal-clear water. And now she didn't know which end was up. Had God changed? Or had she?

Nonie seemed to be waiting for an answer Caley didn't have to give. She sighed. "I'll try, Nonie." That was the best she could do. If she could even do it.

"You know, dear, following your heart doesn't have to mean an adrenaline rush." Nonie peered at Caley as if attempting to see inside her head. "Putting down roots here in Broken Bend—with Brady—just might be your biggest adventure yet."

"I don't know. Maybe." But it wasn't that simple.

Everyone probably thought Mom was sure when she married Dad, and Caley knew all too well how that worked out. How could anyone really know?

Speaking of her parents... She inhaled slightly for courage, finally feeling able to form the statement she'd been debating the entire drive over. "Nonie? I'm...I'm ready." Ready to know the truth. Ready to hear whatever Nonie had hinted at during her last visit before her stop at the cemetery.

Ready to confront the skeletons of the past once and for all.

Nonie kept rocking, as if Caley hadn't just put her entire soul into that simple sentence. "Ready? But Bingo just got comfortable."

Caley frowned before the realization finally sank in. "You named the proverbial elephant Bingo?"

"Well, he didn't seem to be going anywhere." She shot Caley a wink before shifting slightly in the chair to face her.

She snorted. "Then consider me here and armed with elephant spray." She couldn't shake the dry tone of her voice, but from the saucy smile lighting Nonie's face, she knew her grandmother enjoyed the banter.

A faraway expression slowly crossed over Nonie's face, and she closed her eyes as the sun bathed her features. "Do you remember what you told your father that night?"

Caley didn't have to ask which night she meant—the night she told her dad about signing up with the Peace Corps. She slowly shook her head. "I just remember I told him about enlisting, and he freaked out." To put it mildly. She could still hear him yelling in her mind, despite not being able to pull out the specific words. Probably for the best.

Nonie nodded, eyes still closed as if shutting out the present offered a clearer view of the past. "You told him 'I need more than this.'"

That was right. She'd said that after he asked what was so wrong with living at home and going to community college after graduation. "I remember now."

Nonie turned her head until her gaze locked with Caley's. "Tell me what you know about your mother."

She jerked at the abrupt change of subject, the growing pit in her stomach letting her know that maybe it wasn't that big of a switch after all. She petted Scooter with her foot as she sought to put into words the limited knowledge she had of her mom. "I know Mom left us for another man. Some rich guy." That was about all she'd caught in those early years of her dad's mutterings before he shut down the topic completely. "And that she and Dad were high-school sweethearts. I assumed Mom married before she knew what she really wanted in a husband."

"Is that why you haven't settled down yet?"

Caley looked away on impulse, despite knowing Nonie's piercing stare wouldn't miss a thing. "A little." She inhaled the scent of autumn as she fought back unexpected tears. "I don't want to make the same mistakes she did, leave the same trail of pain. I don't want to be like her."

If she was careful about anything in her life, it was that. She might live for taking risks and putting herself on the line for others, but she would never be so selfish that she'd chance destroying her future family the way her mother had destroyed theirs.

Nonie lifted her hand in a brief wave as a fellow resident shuffled past them on a walker, then reached across the chair to grasp Caley's arm. "Your mother didn't just leave for another man. She left for another life."

Caley withdrew from her grip, cracking the tension from her knuckles. "What do you mean?" Her stomach ached, and somehow, she knew her grandmother's next words would matter. A lot.

"When she told your dad she was leaving, do you know what she said?"

No. But as the ache spread, Caley did know. She glanced at Nonie, pain needling her temples, and silently begged her not to confess what she now felt in her heart. But it was like trying to stop a roaring brush fire with a child's bucket full of water.

Nonie's lipstick-tinted mouth pursed before spreading into a thin line. "She said 'I need more than this.'"

Caley eased her truck back onto the road, swiping at the moisture that still puddled under her lids. She'd pulled over as the tears refused to cease on her way home. Nonie's admission and the truth of what she'd put her father through so long ago wouldn't ease up on her conscience, and she almost pulled over a second time to gain control.

Her pager beeped from her hip, but she didn't even glance at it as she continued to drive and relive the past, one heartbreaking memory at a time. She'd wounded her father in a way she'd never understood. No wonder they'd been so strained after that night. But why hadn't he told her? According to Nonie, it was simply because he tried to spare her the truth about her mom. Spare her more pain from the abandonment. It was easier to put it all on himself, and not reveal the whole picture. Her mom hadn't wanted the other man, she wanted what he could give her—everything Caley's dad couldn't. Travel. Money. A world beyond county borders.

Everything Caley had wanted and shoved in her dad's face, too.

She beat the steering wheel with her fist. All these years, she'd sacrificed over and over in an effort not to repeat her mother's mistakes. Yet she'd been far too late.

She was her mother.

Caley pulled into the ranch driveway, skipping her house and going straight to Brady's. They had to talk. Now. Before she stayed on this roller coaster a second longer and risked hurting more people. Despite that kiss, nothing had changed between her and Brady on the surface. She would still be moving on eventually, and they were still miles apart in all the ways it mattered most.

And now she knew for sure she was capable of causing deadly hurricanes in her path.

She jumped out of the truck, ripping the keys from the ignition, and pounded inside the house, almost forgetting to knock. "Brady!" But wait, what was she thinking? He wouldn't be inside. He was never inside.

She changed directions to the barn, Scooter on her heels, and stopped short as she stepped inside the cool interior. The sight of a happy Ava in front of the filly's stall nearly wrenched her heart in two. This would be the hardest sacrifice she'd ever made. But she had to do it. Had to cut and bail now before more people got hurt.

Before more hearts got broken.

She forced a smile at Ava, who grinned and waved wildly. "Come see my filly, Miss Caley! Dad said you already knew about her. Isn't it the coolest?"

"Totally." She projected her voice to be heard down the barn aisle. "But I need to holler at your dad real quick. I'll be right back, okay?" After she talked to Brady.

After she quit her nanny position.

She backpedaled out of the barn before Ava could protest, though the girl looked so entranced by her new pet she doubted she would have anyway. She spun around and caught sight of Brady rounding the corner of her truck.

"You're back! Did you see Ava yet? You were right, she was so— Hey, are you okay?" His grin faded as he took her in. If her burning eyes were any indication, she was probably flushed red from forehead to neck.

She shook her head, directing Scooter into the bed of the truck with a pointed finger and quick word. Part of her wanted to just deny the entire past hour had ever happened, and run into Brady's arms. Pretend like she was really home. Pretend like his hug could erase the revelations from her past. But she couldn't play games. He didn't deserve that, and neither did Ava. No, this needed to be quick. Like removing a Band-Aid.

Brady frowned as he drew closer. "You never park in the back. What's wrong?" His expression paled, and he yanked off his cowboy hat. "Is it Nonie?"

"Nonie's fine. Better than ever." She wished the same could be said for herself. It felt like her dad had died all over again, and this time, it was on her hands. She stifled a sob. "I just got some news, and—I'm sorry, I can't work for you anymore."

She started to open the door of her truck, but Brady quickly stepped in her way. "What are you talking about? What news?" Shock flickered through his eyes before his jaw set. "Did the fire department call? Are you hired?"

It would be easier to let him think that. But she wouldn't lie outright. "I just can't do this anymore, okay?" She reached for the door handle but he once again stepped between her and her means of escape. "Move. Please."

"Caley. I don't understand." He stepped aside, but only a half inch, while his voice, heart-wrenchingly soft, threatened to dissipate her resolve. "What's this really about?" He hesitated. "Was it the kiss?"

Yes. But not in the way he feared. She shook her head. "This is about me. Not us." She averted her eyes, willing herself to hold back the tears until she could make it safely to her own pillow. She couldn't tell him the truth, hated admitting it even to herself. Besides, what she was supposed to say? *I'm more like my mom than I realized? Save yourself while you still can?*

He beat his cowboy hat against his leg. "You're just going to walk away? Quit, just like that? We had an agreement."

Was that all he was concerned about? Losing his laundry folder and less-than-stellar cook? They didn't need her. After the breakthrough he'd had with Ava, they'd be fine on their own. The way Brady had always preferred it.

The way it had to be.

She swallowed everything she wanted to say but couldn't, and gritted her teeth. "Please move."

He held her gaze for a long time, and she wondered which of her own emotions were reflected in his searching stare. Regret. Confusion. Hurt. He finally stepped aside, gesturing grandly to her truck. "Fine. I won't stand in your way."

Oh, but he already had. In all the ways that would permanently brand her heart. She wrenched open the door and climbed into the cab just as Ava jogged out of the barn.

"Miss Caley!" She ran over to them, breathless and grinning, hair flapping in the wind. "Where are you going? Aren't you going to stay for supper?" Her smile vanished as she looked from Caley to her father and back again. "What's going on? Are you crying?"

On the inside, and soon to be on the outside if she didn't get out of there. Caley swallowed back the tears building in her throat. "I've got to go home." Her heart cried a protest that she already was home. From the bed of the truck, Scooter barked, and Caley flinched. Time to go, before the traitorous dog leaped to the ground to stay with Ava. She started the engine.

Ava crossed her arms over her chest, the move appearing more protective than defensive. A frown furrowed her brows. "Will you be back later?"

Caley just shook her head as the first of the tears began to drip. Who had she been kidding? This Band-Aid stuff didn't work at all.

"It's all my fault, isn't it?" Ava's voice rose in pitch and cracked. Tears of her own slipped down her cheeks as she shook her head wildly. "I knew I shouldn't have pulled that stunt with dinner. I tried to set you guys up, and this is what happened."

"Ava, no." Caley reached for her from the open door of her truck, but Ava ducked away.

"I ruin everything." She pressed a shaky hand against her mouth and, with a muffled sob, turned on her heel and rushed toward the pasture.

Caley started to slide from the cab to go after her, but Brady held up one hand, effectively stopping her. "You've done enough. Just leave." His mouth pressed into a straight line. "That's apparently your specialty."

Chapter Nineteen

Hadn't he said Caley Foster was going to be trouble the first day he met her? And now look. She'd somehow not only managed to tear him and his daughter further apart, she'd managed to put them back together again. Shuffle the pieces into a new puzzle and connect them just right. Then up and leave with a moment's notice, keeping one puzzle piece in her pocket as she went.

The one containing his heart.

Brady stared across the pasture in the direction Ava had run, torn between giving her that newfound space and trusting her with responsibility—and wanting to go after her to make sure she didn't get lost in the back woods or stumble too close to Spitfire's pen. But physical safety or not, he couldn't let her go on thinking she'd been the reason for Caley's sudden departure.

He still wasn't even sure what that reason was.

He braced one booted foot on the rail of the fence and rubbed the weathered wood with his palms. Caley's words replayed in his head. *I just got some news. This is about me.* In hindsight, it was clear she was hurting, and reacting from that hurt like an injured animal would. And he certainly hadn't made things better, spouting off about how leaving was her specialty. Man, how could he have said that?

He bit back a groan and leaned down until his forehead touched the top rail. What a mess. Did he go after Caley or give her the space she thought she needed? Earlier he told Max he was backing off after that kiss, for their own good. But that didn't mean he wanted things to end like this. Not when he had yet to get a solid grasp on his own plan of staying friends only. Maybe a fast break of their relationship—employer/employee, friends or more, whatever it was—would be for the best.

But it felt so wrong.

Watching Caley drive away, knowing that might be the last time he saw her, threatened to rip him in half. He wasn't ready for this. No, she wouldn't get away that easily. He at least owed her an apology.

He slowly stood, dragging his boot off the bottom rail, and trudged toward the barn as though his feet had been replaced with anvils. Time to saddle up and go after Ava. Put out one fire, so to speak, before figuring out how to douse another.

And figure out how to douse the love for a certain blonde firefighter still stubbornly igniting in his heart.

Caley lay beside Scooter on her mattress in her room, absently stroking his back. He whined his appreciation and curled up tighter against her torso. "At least I haven't run you off." She tickled his ears the way he liked, half smiling at his responding leg thump.

Her pager beeped, and she pulled it from her pocket and glimpsed the scrolling text. A reminder of the burn ban enforcement. She scrolled to the previous message, and winced. She'd never responded to the page she'd received hours ago on her way home from visiting Nonie, and it'd been a big brush fire not far from the Double C Ranch. Great. Her good standing at the station might have just downgraded several notches. If she didn't get hired on at the department, what would she do?

Was it time to go again?

She glanced at her empty suitcase standing guard near the closet door, which held several boxes leftover from moving that she'd folded and stashed inside. Within minutes, the boxes and that suitcase could be full and she could be on her way again. Just her and Scooter and the open road, leaving behind a failed adventure.

Leaving behind the relentless hurt.

But did she want to be that kind of woman again? The kind who ran when things got hard? The kind who stayed away when love demanded a fight?

An image of Brady and Ava flashed through her mind, and she knew without a doubt it was love—for both of them. She hadn't known their mismatched twosome of a family for long, but she loved them. Despite their quirks and failures and baggage, she knew her feelings as surely as she knew the water ratio of the local fire hydrants based on color. She also knew she'd been put in their lives for a reason.

But was it really only temporarily after all?

She closed her eyes, snuggling Scooter closer. Nonie had told her that putting down roots could be her greatest adventure yet. But how could she be sure she wouldn't turn out even more like her mother than she already was? Wasn't it best to leave Ava and Brady now, rather than realize she couldn't handle Broken Bend indefinitely and leave later, hurting them deeper?

She tried to imagine herself staying in Broken Bend permanently. Staying close to Nonie. Close to Brady and Ava. And even Max, who'd grown on her.

Close to her father's grave.

A fresh wave of pain washed over her, and she shifted on the mattress, nearly knocking Scooter off the side. He barked and repositioned himself, his shuffling legs disturbing the pile of books she kept on the floor by the mattress. Her Bible lay on the bottom.

She gently stroked the leather cover, running her finger over her name that Nonie had engraved before giving it to her in her senior year of high school. She hadn't read it much after college, and maybe that was part of her problem. Maybe that's why she felt so aimless. When she was a senior and studying God's word on a regular basis, she felt led to the Peace Corps. Led to make a difference. It rose above her simple desire to get out of Broken Bend, meant more to her heart than just leaving. It meant being a part of something bigger than herself, meant letting go of the past that kept her chained and setting her free on a worthy adventure.

Maybe that was why she'd been so crushed her dad hadn't reacted as she'd hoped. Not expected, but hoped. And Nonie—well, after watching Brady and Ava, she knew why Nonie had stuck to her son's side. She didn't want Caley to go any more than her dad had. But deep down, Caley knew she'd had Nonie's support, vocal or not, her entire life. She shouldn't have needed it in writing to feel it, believe in it. Nonie had said weeks ago that she never saw an invitation to the graduation ceremony. She'd have come. Caley knew better. Whether it was a mail mix-up or her father had purposefully kept it from her, that wasn't Nonie's fault.

She let the silky-edged pages of the Bible fan through her fingers. Her grandmother had been her rock her entire life—and introduced her as a child to the only sure foundation she'd ever have.

It was Caley who left the solid rock to go sink in quicksand.

She couldn't keep doing this—running from the past, hitting job after job and city after city in hopes the guilt over her unreconciled relationship with her dad wouldn't catch up to her. It'd caught her, all right, and gripped her by the throat.

She could struggle and run again—or she could let it go. Give it to the one who promised in His word He would never leave her nor forsake her. Even if her mother had. And even if Caley had sort of, however unintentionally, done the same thing to her father.

Her dad had let her down, and vice versa. But one thing remained different about her relationship with God compared to that with her earthly father—she would let God down, but He couldn't do the same to her. He was consistent. Forever. Unchanging.

She just had to stand still long enough to let that truth wash over her.

Caley closed her eyes, one hand on Scooter's back, the other resting on top of her Bible. She still didn't have all the answers. But she knew the one who did, and somehow, it would all work out.

She slept peacefully for the first time in years.

Once again, Brady couldn't sleep because of Caley. He paced his bedroom, then the kitchen and finally his barn before wandering outside to roam under the stars. He couldn't help but remember the last time he'd taken a late-night walk and found Caley on her roof. At the time he thought she'd been crazy. Now, the image of her sitting on her roof under a nighttime sky felt right. Natural. That was Caley.

It didn't scare him nearly as much as it had that evening.

And that fact scared him most of all.

He ran his hand over his hair. At least Ava was safe in bed. He'd rounded her up from the pasture, where he'd found her crying at the base of an old oak near the spot where they'd had their picnic with Caley. They'd sat and talked for half an hour before he'd finally convinced Ava that Caley's leaving wasn't her fault. He still wasn't certain she fully believed it.

After what felt like forever trying to convince

Ava her matchmaking schemes hadn't turned Caley away, Ava finally sagged against his chest and said she'd handle it. He assumed that meant she'd talk to Caley herself, which actually wasn't a bad idea. One way or another, he had to figure out what had set Caley off. What could have possibly happened at the nursing home or on the way back to send her into emotional hysterics? Caley wasn't prone to overreacting. Prone to risk taking, yes, but not unmerited drama.

The dry grass crunched under his feet, and in the distance, a hazy fog hung against the black sky, remnants from the brush fire they'd had a few miles away earlier that afternoon. He'd assumed Caley had worked it after seeing it on the news, but she'd shown up at the ranch not long after it'd made the evening report. He had to admit, seeing her rush out of the barn in civilian clothes and not covered in ash gave him more relief than he'd imagined.

One thing was certain—whether Caley left or not, it was far too late to stop caring about her.

He looked in the direction of her rental house, wondering if he should go knock on her door and apologize now. If he woke her up, he'd just apologize for that, too. He couldn't take the constant conversation in his head with her much longer. He needed to speak to her in person, now. Before he lost the courage to make one last stand.

He purposefully started in the direction of her house, then drew up short as the wind shifted. Smoke assaulted his nostrils, and he frowned. The brush fire had been over for hours, and he hadn't smelled it when he'd come outside. This smelled fresh. Hot.

Like the flames dancing in Caley's front yard. Fire.

He stiffened as if electrocuted, panic marring his senses. Caley. He had to warn her. Did she know? But how could he reach her front door with the flames already in her yard? He ventured closer, the flickering strips of orange and gold hypnotizing him with their dance. Suddenly he was a preteen again, stuck in that basement as the walls seemed to melt before his eyes. Trapped. Sweating. Doomed.

The wind changed again, and a rush of cool breeze drifted across his neck, coaxing him out of the past and back into the present. Where Caley needed him. He grabbed his pocket for his phone but only came up with lint. Why hadn't he grabbed his cell? He had to warn Caley, but he also had to call the fire department before the fire reached her house.

He hopped the fence separating their properties as the fire inched closer to the structure. Running wide, he circled around the fire and banged on her front window, unsure which one led to her bedroom. "Caley!" He yelled as loud as he could. "There's a fire! Wake up!" He pounded again even as the back of his shirt warmed. The fire was close. Too close. "Caley!" He beat until he thought the window would shatter.

He heard scuffling inside, followed by loud thuds. She was up. Moving. "I'm coming out the back!"

Her responding yell nearly melted his insides with relief. He backed away from the flames just as they latched on to the house. Like a greedy monster, the fire crept up the wooden trim and toward the roof.

He had to call the fire department and he had no way of knowing if Caley would have her phone on her when she came out. He looked toward the backyard, where she had yet to emerge, hesitating. He didn't want to leave her. But her house was about to be a complete goner. Caley was a firefighter. She knew what to do to take care of herself. Now he needed to do what he could to take care of the rest. Brady made a quick decision.

And ran as fast as he could back to the ranch.

Standing away from the fire at a safe distance down her driveway, Caley crossed her sweatshirt-clad arms over her chest and stared at the flames engulfing her house. She almost laughed from the irony of it all. It was either laugh or cry. A firefighter's house on fire. Wonder what the chief would say about that? She couldn't imagine what they thought when they received her 9-1-1 call and realized whose address it was. How embarrassing.

Then reality sucker-punched her in the stomach. Everything she owned was about to be fried. She didn't have many possessions in the world, but everything she did have was now burning to a crisp. Nonie's blankets. Her favorite firefighter art. All those Christmas ornaments.

Frustration balled in her throat and she clenched her hands into fists. If only she had her gear, she could rush back in before it was too late and grab a few mementos. Suddenly Chief's rule about volunteer gear staying at the station didn't make nearly as much sense as it had before.

"Caley!" Brady's panicked voice echoed across the yard, above the crackle of the flames. He rushed toward her, eyes wide with fear beneath his cowboy hat. "Caley! Where's Ava?"

"What do you mean?" Her heart stammered a half beat before stopping completely. Then it crashed against her rib cage with adrenaline-laced fury. Only this time the familiar rush wasn't welcome. It flat out hurt. "She's at home. Right?" Even as she spoke the words she knew they must not be true, or Brady wouldn't be freaking out.

He held his phone against his ear even as he spoke to her. "I called the fire department in case you couldn't, then went to wake Ava so she would know what was going on. But she wasn't in bed. I'm calling the house phone now over and over. She's not there."

Caley's stomach flipped. "That's impossible. Where else would she go?"

They both stared in dismay at the house, and Brady shook his head. "No way. Ava would never run into a fire."

Sudden, frenzied barking filled the air, and Caley gasped. "Scooter. Where's Scooter? He was right behind me when I left the house!" She searched the ground around her in vain. Despite the nighttime shadows, the fire provided plenty of light. Scooter wasn't there.

And neither was Ava.

Brady paled, the flickering flames creating ghostly shadows against his face. "It's coming from inside."

Caley listened again, forcing her racing pulse to calm so she could hear clearly over her erratic heartbeat. As she stilled and listened, a shadow passed in front of the living room curtains. The unforgiving truth slapped her like a palm across the face. "Ava's inside with Scooter."

Brady stumbled back a step, speechless. Caley didn't allow herself the luxury of thinking. She plucked Brady's hat off his head and settled it onto her own, then tugged her sweatshirt sleeves down over her hands and ran.

Straight toward the flames.

Brady watched the scene before him, numb, as if viewing a movie. His eyes took in the facts but his mind refused to comprehend it all. Caley, snatching his hat and taking off toward the house—toward the fire that licked the roof as if it was a child's lollipop. The shadows passing in front of the window, then disappearing, Scooter barking so ferociously it was a wonder the dog hadn't gone hoarse. Facts. Happening to someone else. In some other time.

Then with a rush, the truth filtered through his foggy brain. The two people he loved more than anyone else in the world were inside a burning house. And he stood in the yard, once again failing those who depended on him. Needed him. Caley was a firefighter, but she had no gear. What could she do that he couldn't? He didn't know, but he did know the panicked weight on his chest would be nothing compared to the load he'd carry if anything happened to either of them.

Yet his feet remained planted in the yard as if his boots had been filled with concrete. The house blurred in his vision and changed shapes, taking him back to the basement of his nightmares. The dim corners, lit only with golden-yellow and rust-colored flames. The smoke-filled darkness, choking off his screams for help. The basement window he'd smashed with a brick.

The fireman's face suddenly filling that small screen, hollering words of encouragement before Brady collapsed.

Why hadn't he remembered that part before? The fireman? He'd blocked it out, only remembering the fear. The panic. The adrenaline rush that burned his veins. That fireman had saved his life. If he hadn't broken that window, they wouldn't have found him until it was too late. That fireman had been his rescue. His hope during a consuming fire.

Just like the pastor at church had preached about God. *Grateful for this security…for our God is a consuming fire….*

Security. Trust. Faith.

Caley should have been out by now.

He might not have come through for his wife. But he had to come through for his daughter—and for the woman who'd stolen the heart he didn't know could still beat.

"God, help me." He breathed the words through teeth gritted with fear. But his muscles awakened with strength, and life flowed through his veins. He wasn't alone. He could do this.

Or he'd die trying.

Determination pushed him through the flames.

He dropped immediately to the ground in the smoke-filled room and tore at his work shirt, grateful for the thick material. The buttons popped free and he held the shirt around his nose as he army-crawled over the shaggy carpet, the heat so intense his eyes watered.

"Caley! Ava!" His voice didn't carry nearly as far as he'd hoped, and he coughed and tried again. "Caley!"

More barking, from the direction of the kitchen, if he remembered correctly. He changed direction, wincing as he bumped his head against what had to be the futon. He kept going. "Ava! Caley!"

The silence, save for the steady crackle of flames, began to bring back the dark memories. No. Not now. He couldn't afford a panic attack, not when Caley and Ava depended on him. He sent up another prayer, clinging to the fact that God could see through the smoke even when he couldn't. *God, You're here. You have to be. I have no other hope. Please guide me. Don't let me fail again.*

Then Scooter barked, the Lab's voice finally dying out in rasps. Suddenly, the dog appeared through the smoke, directly in front of him, tail wagging. He licked Brady's cheek and whined deep in his throat, as if urging him forward. Brady crawled faster, his hands finding the cool tile of the kitchen floor. "Caley?"

"We're over here." Caley's weak, muffled voice

sounded to his left, and he reached blindly until his hand grasped her jeans-clad leg. "I got turned around, and the smoke...I couldn't leave Ava."

"We'll get out. I promise." He held on tight, unwilling to let her go, feeling with his free hand for Ava until he drew close enough to see her pale face, eyes closed. His heart skipped.

"She's breathing. But we have to get out of this smoke." Caley coughed, the harsh sound progressing until she gagged. Brady stood up, clutching the shirt to his nose, and felt along the counter. Metal. Faucet. The sink. He turned on the water and wet the shirt, then handed it to Caley. "Cover Ava's nose and mouth."

Where was the fire department? They had to get out, get fresh air. But going back through the living room was too risky. They'd both gotten confused once already. So what was left? The window? It might be their only chance. A sudden roar filled the air above them. The roof.

Brady's question was answered. They were leaving. Now.

He ripped open drawers until he felt a dish towel, wrapped it around his fist and felt for the window. He held his breath and punched as hard as he could. Pain radiated up his fist and into his forearm, but the answering shatter of glass and the responding rush of fresh air numbed the hurt.

He knocked out the shards around the edges of the frame and dropped the towel to the floor.

"Caley!"

As if they'd practiced this procedure a hundred times, she suddenly appeared at his elbow. Without a word, he gripped her waist and hoisted her up, then lowered her through the window. Once she hit bottom, he reached down and scooped up Ava's limp form. With another prayer on his lips, he leaned out the window until he could deposit Ava into Caley's waiting arms. She staggered away with her, nearly falling before steadying herself and dashing across the grass toward safety. Brady grabbed Scooter before slipping out the window himself.

"Good dog." He set the Lab on the ground, and together they rushed to Ava's side, where Caley bathed her face with his wet shirt.

Brady clutched Ava's hand. "She going to be okay?" His throat burned and his chest grew tight from the effects of the smoke. He could only imagine how ragged Caley felt. Black soot streaked her face and covered her sweatshirt, along with more than one spot where the fabric had completely burned away.

She leaned down close, fingers checking for Ava's pulse. "She needs oxygen and an IV. But yes." The words left Caley's throat in little more than a rough whisper, but she never looked up from her patient. She probably needed the exact same treatment, but she'd never admit it. She was being a hero, just like she'd been taught.

And she'd never looked more beautiful doing what she did best.

Behind them, the roof collapsed, finally surrendering to the fire's power. A burst of black smoke spiraled through the air. Then sirens, blessed sirens, filled the night with their high-pitched wail.

Brady collapsed against the grass, his weary chest heaving. Grass blades scratched his bare back, but nothing had ever felt so good. So normal. "We're safe, girls. We're safe."

He closed his eyes, gritty and dry, and gulped a breath of fresh air. Despite the lingering worry over Ava, an indescribable peace washed over his spirit.

He'd left behind one fire—and surrendered to another.

Chapter Twenty

Caley reached up to rub her eyes, which felt coated with sand, and frowned at the IV stuck in the top of her hand. "This wasn't necessary." She hated IVs, had since she was a kid.

Brady, wearing an oversized T-shirt the hospital had given him, since his work shirt had been ruined, scooted his chair closer to her cot in the E.R. The nurses, due to lack of space and Brady's cowboy charm and candy-coated pleas, had agreed to let her and Ava share an E.R. curtain so Brady wouldn't have to go back and forth between them. "You inhaled as much smoke as Ava. You're just better conditioned."

She didn't feel very conditioned. She felt weak, tired and hot, despite the air-conditioner vent blowing straight on her. And her throat felt as if the fire still lingered inside. "Water." She was grumpy, now, too, and couldn't figure out why she kept fighting back tears. Unless the relief had gotten to her.

Brady handed her the plastic cup the nurse had provided, and she gulped down several mouthfuls of water.

"Is Ava okay?" She glanced at her young roommate, the girl's blond hair splayed against the pillow as she slept. Ava had woken up earlier, after being treated, and then immediately fell back asleep while they waited to admit her. The doctor wanted to keep Ava overnight as a precaution and do an X-ray on her lungs the next morning to make sure there wasn't more damage.

Caley's stare lingered, taking in every inch of the girl she'd almost lost. They both needed showers, as evidenced by the soot still marring her fair complexion. Although, now, Caley had nowhere *to* shower. The reality of her situation struck hard, and was no match for the tears begging to fall.

"That's the third time you've asked about Ava in thirty minutes." He smiled, taking the impatience out of his words. His grin vanished as rogue tears slipped down her cheeks. "Of course she's going to be okay. Thanks to you."

"And you." Caley reached for Brady's hand, her unsteady tidal wave of emotion threatening to topple her right off the bed. She sniffed, the familiar smells of hospital antiseptic and latex gloves filling her senses. Except she was used to being on the other side of the IV. She gripped his hand tighter. "You really came through."

"You ran into the fire first."

She shrugged. "I've been trained to do that."

"Not without bunker gear." Brady lifted his eyebrow at her.

Good point.

Beside them, Ava stirred, her eyes fluttering open. She shifted in the bed, then sat upright, the thin mattress squeaking under her small frame.

"Easy, there, kid." Brady instantly moved to her side, grabbing her bottle of water and pressing it into her hands as he steadied her. "Take some sips before you talk."

Seeing her dad, Ava's panicked expression relaxed. She drank greedily before handing the nearly empty bottle back to him.

"Better?" He twisted the lid back on.

She nodded, pressing her hand against her throat. "It hurts."

"Don't talk right now, sweetie. You're going to stay here overnight, but it will be okay. I'm staying with you."

"So am I." The words flew from Caley's lips before she could consider if she was intruding. But from Brady's immediate nod, she knew she wasn't. Besides, she couldn't imagine leaving Ava's side right now. Not after what they'd been through together.

And she had nowhere else to go.

"I'm sorry." Tears filled Ava's eyes, and Brady, still bent over her in concern, wiped them away with his finger. "It's my fault."

He straightened, pulling back to see her face. "The fire? No, honey. The firemen said it was sparks from the brush fire they extinguished earlier in the day. The wind carried it over. You didn't do it."

"No, not the fire. Getting hurt." Ava's trembling hand, topped with her own IV, pointed at Caley. "I hid in your house because I wanted to talk to you." She paused as a series of coughs choked her voice. "I came through the back door, but you were asleep. So I lay down in the living room to wait and must have fallen asleep, too. When I woke up…" Her tired voice trailed to a hoarse rasp. "The smoke…"

Caley reached across the small space between them on the cots and squeezed Ava's hand, mindful of their IVs. "No. It was my fault for leaving like I did. I was upset. It was only normal you wanted to come see me." She should have known better, and now she could kick herself for behaving so foolishly. Of course announcing her departure so suddenly would upset Ava. But she'd never have imagined she'd try to sneak over on her own later that night. She'd underestimated how much Ava cared. The thought both warmed her heart and chilled her to the bone. The night's events could have turned out so much differently.

"It's understandable, but you do know better than to sneak out at night." Brady's voice, firm but gentle, rose above Caley's. "Bad things can happen."

"I know that now." Ava rolled her eyes, and Caley bit back a relieved grin at the preteen frustration. She was definitely going to be okay. "I won't do it again. I promise."

"You know who really saved the day?" Caley let go of Ava's hand and eased back against her pillows. Ava did the same, as if suddenly remembering how exhausted she was. "Scooter. He barked the entire time you were inside until I got there. Then he barked the entire time until your dad got there."

"Is he okay?" Worry seeped onto her face, and she stiffened on the bed.

Brady nodded. "Uncle Max took him to the vet. But he'll be just fine."

A small grin crept across Ava's face. "He's a hero." Her expression sobered. "So are you, Miss Caley. And you, Dad." She reached up her skinny arms, and Brady pulled her into his embrace.

"I love you." He whispered the words against her hair, and Ava nestled into his hug.

"I love you, too."

Caley teared up again watching the heartfelt

scene before her, even as a sharp pain reminded her that she wasn't a part of it. Not truly. This was their moment, and while she took great joy in knowing she'd helped bring the father-daughter duo back together, it was still a duo.

Not a trio.

Ava folded her thin pillow so it was thicker, and rolled over on her side. "I think I'm going to nap until they get my room ready."

"Good idea." Brady brushed her hair back from her forehead. "We'll get you cleaned up soon, too. I promise. You'll feel better after a shower."

She nodded, eyes fluttering closed. Within moments her breathing grew deep and even. Caley listened hard, grateful she couldn't hear any wheezing from the girl's lungs. Hopefully she'd get good results on her X-ray and get to go home tomorrow.

Brady smoothed back Ava's hair, then, instead of returning to his chair, came over and perched on the side of Caley's bed. "Speaking of heroes…" He grasped her hand. "There's something you need to know."

"That I'm too big of a risk taker and out of your league?" The snarky response stemmed from her personal hurt and stress, and she bit her tongue. He didn't deserve that. It wasn't his fault she was who she was.

Though staring into his eyes, she wasn't sure

she wanted to be that same girl anymore. She wanted to be his girl.

"No. That you're a risk taker, and I love you. Just the way you are."

The words slid over her weary body like a healing balm. But however much she longed to hear those words from him, they weren't true. Not really. She'd seen people speak their hearts during a tragedy, then change their minds the minute life returned to normal. It was human nature.

She briefly closed her eyes before reaching up to touch his cheek. "You're just saying that because of tonight. You'll change your mind tomorrow." Above them the hospital speakers squawked, paging a doctor. Around them, life continued, hustling on, proving Caley's point. This was an emotionally charged night. Nothing more.

Even though she longed for it to be.

"No, I'm serious. I had a wake-up call." He took a deep breath, lacing his fingers through hers. "When I saw you run into that fire, risking your life for my daughter, it changed everything inside me. It still makes me nervous, but the world needs people like you, Caley. And people like the fireman who saved me from that burning basement years ago. Without people like that, I wouldn't be here." He swallowed hard, his Adam's apple bobbing in his throat. "Without people like you, Ava wouldn't be here."

He meant it. She could see the love in his eyes. But it still felt too good to be true. She studied their entwined fingers, relishing the safety in those hands. The sparks. The love. She gingerly met his gaze. "I realized sort of the opposite."

"What do you mean?" He shifted beside her, scooting closer to reach up with his free hand and tuck her hair behind her ear.

His touch against her face made her flush even hotter, and this time it wasn't from the memories of the fire. "That some risks are worth it. And others aren't." She shrugged. "I've done a lot of things and accomplished a lot of goals in my life. Crazy stuff that meant a lot to me at the time. But now…" Her voice trailed off, and she coughed. Her raw throat hurt like anything, but she had to get this out. "I think the one thing I want the most will be the biggest risk for me yet."

"What's that?"

She met his gaze full on. "A forever home."

Hope filled his eyes. "So no more running?"

"I'm tired of running. Tired of job-hopping and never knowing what's coming next. I thrived on that for a long time, but now, after realizing how much you and Ava mean to me…" Caley shook her head. "Leaving doesn't seem like a choice anymore. And Nonie still needs me. I can't abandon her, either." She inhaled deeply, offering a half smile. "For the first time in my entire life, Broken Bend feels like it could really be home."

"I'd like that." Brady's husky voice warmed her to the core. "Are you sure, Caley?"

"Positive." Peace flooded her senses. For once, the thought of staying put didn't bring anxiety and a desperate itch to get moving. Nonie had been right. It was time for her biggest adventure yet. And she couldn't wait.

Rubbing her thumb over Brady's knuckles, she smirked. "Something else I know for sure—I'm telling Chief their response time is pretty unacceptable."

"I heard that." Chief Talbot appeared beside the half-closed curtain, his smooth-shaven face turning up in a smile. His teeth shone bright against his tanned face. "Guess it might be time to rethink my rule about volunteer gear remaining at the station, right, Ms. Foster?"

Caley fought her jaw threatening to drop in surprise. Brady edged a little farther from her on the bed, but didn't let go of her hand. She clung to it. "Chief. I was joking, I—"

"No, you're right. It was unacceptable, and lives were in danger." Chief rocked back on his heels, thumbs hooked casually in the pockets of his uniform pants. "The crew was working another brush fire on the far edge of the district when your call came in. We had to request backup, but our men left that fire to come to you as soon as they got word." He shook his head as he peered over Caley at Ava's sleeping form. "I'm just glad things worked out the way they did. You're a hero."

She glanced at Ava, more grateful than she could put into words. But the urge to be a hero didn't consume her anymore. Instead, the feeling was replaced by a maternal desire, to nurture. Grow. Be a rock for someone else, instead of floundering to find one to stand upon, herself. "Thank you, Chief."

"I came by to offer you the job." Chief cleared his throat, jingling the change in his pockets. "It's yours, Ms. Foster. You've already earned it, but tonight just further proves how much of an honor it'd be to have you on the department."

The job was hers. Did she still want it?

Brady let go of her hand to rub her shoulder. "Congrats, Caley! That's great."

But instead of the expected rush of joy and excitement, she felt nothing but a steady assurance prompting her to listen to her heart. And her heart wasn't in it. As much as she loved firefighting, it was time to put aside her own dreams and focus on the people she loved. She owed it to Brady— and more than that, she *wanted* to.

It was time for a change. And this time, the risk would have the biggest payoff yet.

Drawing a breath for courage, she forced a smile

at the chief. "I'm honored, too, sir. But I respectfully decline."

"What?" Brady and Chief Talbot's voice mixed in surprised unison.

Her gaze darted between both of them before landing on Brady. "I've found my true purpose right here."

"Caley. You don't have to do this for me. I told you, I understand now." Brady lowered his voice, and the chief stepped a few paces back in a vain effort to give them privacy. "I trust you. More than that, I trust God." His grin morphed into a wince. "Or at least, I'm trying to."

"You can't change everything overnight, Brady. I know you're still uncomfortable with my job, no matter how much you're trying to convince yourself you're not. Listen—I pick you and Ava." Caley reached up and touched his stubbled cheek. "It's time for me to land."

"But you don't have to choose." He covered her hand with his own, searching her gaze for a long moment. Then he stood to address the chief. "Sir, I wouldn't dare dream of speaking for this woman…" He shot Caley a wink. "And she did say no. But I'm pretty sure that she'd love to continue to volunteer for your department as often as she can."

"Brady McCollough, was that a compromise?"

She narrowed her eyes at him—the rancher next door, the thorn in her side. The love of her life.

"I believe it was."

"Works for me." Chief folded his sturdy arms across his chest. "But if you change your mind, Ms. Foster, please let us know. I hope to see you around the station once you recover."

"You can count on it, sir." She nodded, and he lifted one hand in a wave to them both before slipping around the curtain and disappearing into the hallway bustle.

Brady joined her back on the cot. Beside them, Ava stirred in her sleep, a soft moan in the back of her throat. She was probably dreaming. "I'm sure you're both ready to get home."

"What home?" Caley snorted. The peace of making the right decision for her future temporarily faltered at the memory of what she'd already lost. She squeezed her eyes shut. *God, I know we're a team again. And I know you have a plan. But this still hurts.*

"Actually, you have a pretty awesome home waiting for you." Brady shrugged nonchalantly. "It's a little rough around the edges, needs a woman's touch. And there's this kid that lives upstairs who keeps her room pretty messy." He trailed one finger lightly over her wrist. "But it's got plenty of room."

"Sounds perfect." Caley leaned in, and his

mouth covered hers in a lingering kiss, full of hope. Promise. And adventure.

"Dad."

They broke apart, turning in surprise to see Ava awake. She propped halfway up on her elbows, hair ruffled from sleep. Despite her weary expression, her eyes shone. "Come on. Propose already."

Caley laughed, and Brady grinned before kissing her again. "Sounds like the best idea I've heard in a while."

He knelt down on the hospital floor and took her hands in his. She slid to the edge of the cot before him, her injuries fading to a dull ache as she took in the love in his eyes. Her heart thudded wildly. Talk about an adrenaline rush.

"Caley Foster." He took a deep breath. "You can't cook. You make me more nervous than a cat in a room full of rocking chairs. And I'm pretty sure you're responsible for the gray hairs I found under my hat the other day." He gripped both of her hands in his, holding them like a lifeline, and his grin faded to a serious expression. "But if there's anyone who's going to lie on the roof and count stars, run into a burning house or help me lasso a runaway bull, it's got to be you. I need you in my life. We need you." He nodded at Ava, who grinned so wide her face seemed to glow. "Will you marry me? Marry us?"

Tears filled her eyes again, but this time, they

weren't born of pain or injury. Rather from hope. Joy. Happiness. "Of course I will." She lunged forward, temporarily forgetting her IV and her burns and her smoke-scented hair, and straight into his arms.

He stood up just in time to catch her, hugging her and lifting her off the ground. "I love you."

"I love you, too." She pulled back just far enough to kiss him and seal the deal, while Ava cheered from her cot.

She was finally home.

* * * * *

Dear Reader,

The Rancher Next Door combines two of my favorite careers—ranching and firefighting. There's something so heroic about a fireman risking his life on a regular basis to run into the flames that most would run away from. And there's something just as heroic about a cowboy maintaining and protecting his animals, land and the people he loves most.

Both firemen and cowboys have a reputation of being attractive stereotypes, but as the wife of a fireman/cowboy, I wanted to write this story to show the other side—the pain they experience, the burdens they bear, the struggles they face. Under every cowboy hat lies a set of shoulders loaded with responsibility, and beneath every oxygen tank lies a soul ready to give his life for the greater good.

In this story Brady, a rancher, and Caley, a firefighter, must learn to compromise and share their burdens not only for love of each other, but for young Ava. This means starting from scratch and digging to the depth of the real issues they each face—issues of guilt and regret and the attitude that only they can do it all. At this depth lies a fissure in their faith, born from various reasons and more dangerous than any stampeding bull or roaring fire. They each have to come to terms with how God is truly a consuming fire—and what that means to them personally.

My prayer is that this story will ignite a spark in your own faith, wherever you are on the journey—and prompt you to hug a hero today.

Blessings,

Betsy St. Amant

Questions for Discussion

1. Brady lets what he views as failure to keep his wife safe in the past determine how he over-protects his daughter. Would you react in the same way under similar circumstances? Why or why not?

2. Ava isn't a typical girly-girl and longs to be outside on the ranch with her father. Do you think Ava just wanted to be around the animals or do you think part of her reasoning was to spend time with her dad any way she could? Explain.

3. Caley is used to moving from city to city, place to place. Are you more of a homebody, or do you prefer going and doing constantly? Why?

4. As a female firefighter, Caley is used to a lot of sexist jokes and tension in the workplace. Do you think females in male-dominated career fields are still subject to this? Has America made significant progress in this area of treatment? Why or why not?

5. Brady married young and had a tumultuous first marriage, which also hangs heavily on him after his wife's accident. Do you think

marrying young and quickly increases the odds for divorce in today's time? Why or why not?

6. Why do you feel Ava and Brady's relationship was so strained? What could they have done before Caley's involvement to improve it on their own?

7. Have you ever had a child meddle in your love relationships via matchmaking? Did it work? Why or why not?

8. Caley returned to Broken Bend to restore her relationship with her grandmother, Nonie. Would you ever move somewhere you didn't want to be in order to be there for a family member? Why or why not?

9. Despite Caley's detachment to people and places, she always carries Scooter with her almost everywhere she goes. Have you ever let an animal replace a human friendship in your life? Do you think this is healthy? Why or why not?

10. Caley and Ava have a lot in common—both lost their mothers in different ways at an early age. How do you feel this affects a child dur-

ing their childhood? How does it affect them into adulthood?

11. Brady and Caley both have their own issues with God—Brady because he felt God wasn't in control after all after his wife's accident, and Caley because she received a negative view of what being a dad meant. She confused her earthly father with her heavenly father. Do you think it's common for women from broken homes to do this? How can they maintain a more accurate view of the God who loves them unconditionally?

12. Nonie, despite her fragile health, provides a steady stream of wisdom for Caley during her time in Broken Bend, and is also the source of Caley's coziest memories of childhood. Who has been a mentor for you growing up or made your childhood memories fond?

13. Ava wants Caley to be her stepmother so badly, she risks getting in trouble to set up a special dinner between Caley and Brady. Would you have punished her under the circumstances, or reacted as Caley prompts Brady to react?

14. Caley has been unknowingly running all her life from the past, afraid to let the regrets catch up to her and consume her completely. Have

you ever had a relationship go unreconciled until it was too late? How did/do you handle the pain?

15. Brady fears ranch life is too dangerous for his young daughter, Ava. Do you think he's right or do you feel there is a middle ground he and Ava could have reached a lot sooner?

LARGER-PRINT BOOKS!

GET 2 FREE LARGER-PRINT NOVELS PLUS 2 FREE MYSTERY GIFTS

Love Inspired

Larger-print novels are now available...

LARGER-PRINT BOOKS!

GET 2 FREE LARGER-PRINT NOVELS PLUS 2 FREE MYSTERY GIFTS

Love Inspired®
SUSPENSE
RIVETING INSPIRATIONAL ROMANCE

Larger-print novels are now available...

YES! Please send me 2 FREE LARGER-PRINT Love Inspired® Suspense novels and my 2 FREE mystery gifts (gifts are worth about $10). After receiving them, if I don't wish to receive any more books, I can return the shipping statement marked "cancel." If I don't cancel, I will receive 4 brand-new novels every month and be billed just $4.99 per book in the U.S. or $5.49 per book in Canada. That's a savings of at least 23% off the cover price. It's quite a bargain! Shipping and handling is just 50¢ per book in the U.S. and 75¢ per book in Canada.* I understand that accepting the 2 free books and gifts places me under no obligation to buy anything. I can always return a shipment and cancel at any time. Even if I never buy another book, the two free books and gifts are mine to keep forever.

110/310 IDN FVZ7

Name _____ (PLEASE PRINT) _____

Address _____ Apt. # _____

City _____ State/Prov. _____ Zip/Postal Code _____

Signature (if under 18, a parent or guardian must sign) _____

Mail to the Harlequin® Reader Service:
IN U.S.A.: P.O. Box 1867, Buffalo, NY 14240-1867
IN CANADA: P.O. Box 609, Fort Erie, Ontario L2A 5X3

Are you a current subscriber to Love Inspired Suspense books and want to receive the larger-print edition?
Call 1-800-873-8635 or visit www.ReaderService.com.

* Terms and prices subject to change without notice. Prices do not include applicable taxes. Sales tax applicable in N.Y. Canadian residents will be charged applicable taxes. Offer not valid in Quebec. This offer is limited to one order per household. Not valid for current subscribers to Love Inspired Suspense larger-print books. All orders subject to credit approval. Credit or debit balances in a customer's account(s) may be offset by any other outstanding balance owed by or to the customer. Please allow 4 to 6 weeks for delivery. Offer available while quantities last.

Your Privacy—The Harlequin® Reader Service is committed to protecting your privacy. Our Privacy Policy is available online at www.ReaderService.com or upon request from the Harlequin Reader Service.

We make a portion of our mailing list available to reputable third parties that offer products we believe may interest you. If you prefer that we not exchange your name with third parties, or if you wish to clarify or modify your communication preferences, please visit us at www.ReaderService.com/consumerchoice or write to us at Harlequin Reader Service Preference Service, P.O. Box 9062, Buffalo, NY 14269. Include your complete name and address.

LISLPDIR13

ReaderService.com

Manage your account online!
- Review your order history
- Manage your payments
- Update your address

**We've designed
the Harlequin® Reader Service
website just for you.**

Enjoy all the features!
- Reader excerpts from any series
- Respond to mailings and
  special monthly offers
- Discover new series available to you
- Browse the Bonus Bucks catalog
- Share your feedback

Visit us at:
ReaderService.com